THE ECHOING BELLS

In Germany Marnie Burness accepts the post of governess at Schloss Beissel. Her charge is Count von Oldenburg's daughter, Charlotte. Despite finding much to disapprove of at the Schloss, against her own principles she falls in love with the Count. Then, when Maria, the Count's wife, is murdered Marnie suspects his involvement. She leaves the Schloss, but will she ever learn the truth about the death of the Countess — and will her suspicions of the Count be proved right?

Books by Lillie Holland
in the Linford Romance Library:

LILLIE HOLLAND

THE ECHOING BELLS

Complete and Unabridged

LINFORD
Leicester

First published in Great Britain in 2008

First Linford Edition
published 2009

British Library CIP Data

Holland, Lillie.
  The echoing bells.
  1. Governesses- -Germany- -Fiction.
  2. Countesses- -Germany- -Death- -Fiction.
  3. Love stories. 4. Large type books.
  I. Title
  823.9'2–dc22

  ISBN 978-1-84782-904-7

Published by
F. A. Thorpe (Publishing)
Anstey, Leicestershire

Set by Words & Graphics Ltd.
Anstey, Leicestershire
Printed and bound in Great Britain by
T. J. International Ltd., Padstow, Cornwall

This book is printed on acid-free paper

For Miriam, Sarah, Linda and Eva.

1

I shall never forget the day that Miss Hetherington, our headmistress, sent for me and asked me if I would like to attend finishing school in southern Germany for a couple of years. For a moment my breath was taken away. Excitement rushed through me, but at the same time I thought of my home, and of my aunt and uncle. They had brought me up and loved me from the time both my parents had died in a diphtheria epidemic. I had only been six years old, so they were now just fond memories.

Miss Hetherington went on talking. 'There is a very good school in the Black Forest area. It is highly recommended by Miss Schwele, our German Mistress. What do you think of the idea, Marion?' She always gave me my proper name, although everyone else called me Marnie.

'I would love to go,' I said slowly. 'I would miss my home dreadfully, though. Perhaps too much to bear. My aunt and uncle may not wish me to go either . . . '

My uncle was a medical practitioner with a large number of patients in Southsands. We had a cook-housekeeper, Mrs. McNulty, a housemaid, Tina, and a scullery maid. We had stables at the back of the house, with three horses and a smart trap, and a paddock and orchard. We also had a man, Linton, to look after the stables and the garden. I knew that some of my school friends came from much larger establishments than mine, but as I was very happy at home, I did not envy them.

'You will not be going alone. Isabel Fairclose is going too. I told her not to mention it to you before I did.'

So Isabel Fairclose was going! She was a boarder at Wellyn Girls' School. She was seventeen, the same age as myself, and although we had never been close friends, we had always been on good terms. She was a plump, dark, pretty girl, and I had an idea that her parents were a good deal wealthier than my aunt and uncle.

'You will be company for each other,' said Miss Hetherington. 'School on the Continent will broaden your outlook in many ways. Southsands is a very pleasant town, but it is still just a south coast seaside resort. Even if you were to return and spend the rest of your days here, I do not think that you would regret your time in Germany. By the way, I have already consulted your aunt and uncle, and they are agreeable.'

After that interview, up to the time of our actual departure for Germany, Isabel and I could think and talk of little else. Her parents were taking us there, and then spending some time in Italy before returning to England. Aunt Matilda went with me to choose material for a travelling costume and sundry other things, and we also had a day in London shopping. That trip culminated in a visit to her sister, Alice, who said that I would probably be homesick, and that my aunt and uncle would miss me terribly. She added that young people no longer appreciated their homes. We both felt rather upset when we arrived back at The Elms, as our house was called. I assured my aunt quite truthfully that of course I appreciated my home. We both wept at the prospect of my going away, and Uncle Peter was very quiet and serious-looking as my departure grew close.

When the parting finally came, it had a strangely dreamlike quality, as did my first impressions of Germany. The pine forests, the tinkle of cow-bells, the mountains and the mists and the castles on the hills looked just like the illustrations in my book of fairy stories. The sound and smell of the wind in the fir trees, the dropping fire of huntsmen, the dull stroke of the wood-axe, bad roads, fresh trout for supper in the clean chamber of an inn; all these things delighted me as we travelled to the garrison town of Leiknar in south-west Germany.

The school, a few miles from there, was run by a widowed lady, *Frau* Krafft. It had once been a convent, and was still called the *Damenstift*. It was a stark, somewhat forbidding stone building, and our bedrooms were the narrow cells once occupied by nuns. The pupils were girls of different nationalities, but after the first, strange, homesick weeks had passed, Isabel and I settled down and enjoyed ourselves. I became very fluent in German. We spent Christmas at the *Damenstift*, but went home for the Easter vacation.

My uncle had engaged a young Scots doctor, Alistair Harlow, to assist him in his practice. He was unmarried, his home was in Edinburgh, and he lived in comfortable lodgings in Southsands. We got on well with each other right from the start, and he asked if he might write to me when I went back to Germany. I liked the idea, and we corresponded.

Isabel Fairclose left the *Damenstift*

after only a year. She thought that she had spent long enough at school, and her parents agreed. I myself intended to stay for another twelve months, but shortly before winter turned into spring in my second year there, *Frau* Krafft sent for me.

She told me that the Count and Countess von Oldenburg had applied to her in their search for a new governess for their thirteen-year-old daughter, Charlotte.

'It would be such an honour! For you and for the school! They are such a noble family. The Counts of von Oldenburg have been hereditary rulers of Goppertal and district since mediaeval times. Somebody must have spoken well of my school . . . ' She paused. 'You must apply for this position, Marnie. You are English, you speak excellent German and very good French. What is more, you are very attractive. You have style, elegance.'

'But I might not wish to take it, *Frau* Krafft.'

6

'You have enjoyed helping to teach the younger girls sometimes. You are a born teacher.'

'Even if I applied and got the position, my aunt and uncle are likely to want me at home when I have finished at the *Damenstift*. Why can't they send their daughter here? It's only about twenty miles from Goppertal.'

Frau Krafft threw up her hands in horror. 'No, no! They are aristocrats. You do not understand. She must be educated at home.'

'Very well, *Frau* Krafft. To please you I will go for an interview.'

I understood her attitude towards the von Oldenburgs better when I was met from the train at Goppertal Station and driven up the mountain road to the great, imposing fortress that was Schloss Beissel. I could see the walls with their flanking turrets, and felt almost panic-stricken as the horses climbed higher and higher. In the vast, unwelcoming entrance hall a footman enquired my business, and a young maidservant in an enormous mob-cap took me to her mistress. I was led up the wide staircase, with its balustrade of carved ironwork, and along what seemed to be endless corridors. At last she stopped and knocked on the door of a room. It was opened by a big, untidy-looking woman of about sixty.

'*Fraulein* — er — Burness?' She had a deep, hoarse voice. 'Come this way.'

I followed her into a large and beautifully proportioned room. The chimney piece was richly carved, and the ceiling was painted. The windows were long and narrow, but allowed in plenty of light, showing off the fine gilt chairs and mahogany furniture. A great four-poster bed with heavy gold brocade curtains dominated the room. My glance took in the rumpled pillows and disordered coverlet. I was in the Countess' bedchamber, and it was quite obvious that she had only recently vacated her bed.

A young and very beautiful woman was sitting in a gilt chair in front of the fire. She was wearing a pale green *peignoir*.

'*Fraulein* Burness? Good day. I am Countess von Oldenburg,' she said. 'Be seated.' With an imperious gesture she dismissed the older woman, who withdrew into an adjoining room. I sat down opposite the Countess.

She had masses of amber-coloured hair falling in waves below her waist, and her eyes were almost identical in shade. She had a creamy skin, and a red, pouting mouth. The thin *peignoir* revealed the full curves of her figure.

'You have been attending *Frau* Krafft's school for nearly two years,' she said.

'That is correct.'

'We have heard good reports of that school, and you have been highly recommended for the post of governess to my daughter, Charlotte. She had a very good governess from the age of six, but ill health compelled *Fraulein* Schiller to leave us. She was very strict . . . you understand?'

9

'Yes,' I said, rather doubtfully. 'I am not an experienced governess.'

'That does not matter. *Frau* Krafft says that you have done some teaching at the school, and that you are a natural teacher. Being young, you will be more adaptable. My daughter is being brought up very strictly; she is being prepared for a certain position in life. She speaks French quite well, but we wish her to be fluent in English also. She is inclined to be lazy; she has faults which must be corrected. If she is wilful, she must be punished.'

'Punished? In what way, Your Excellency?' I asked anxiously. This daughter of aristocratic parents did not appear to have a very enviable life.

'Kept to her room, forbidden to speak, forbidden to play, forbidden to eat anything but the plainest food.'

Forbidden, forbidden, forbidden. No, I could not come here and teach this child.

'You will be well paid if you are satisfactory. I would like you to meet my daughter now. I bid you good day, *Fraulein* Burness.' She pronounced my name as they all did in Germany, giving the two syllables equal emphasis, and hissing the sibilants slightly. She rang a silver bell, and the big untidy-looking woman appeared. Despite her careless appearance, she seemed very sure of herself, and I had the impression that she had been in the employment of the von Oldenburgs for a long time. The Countess instructed her to take me to the schoolroom, addressing her as 'Gertrud'.

I was led through another maze of corridors and up some stairs. Gertrud stopped suddenly outside a door. Tapping on it, she called out: '*Fraulein* Charlotte!'

We entered a large, somewhat bare room. The floor was covered with worn green linoleum, and there was a desk, a blackboard and a large table. There was also a bookcase, several chairs and a piano. A young girl was sitting beside the fire with an open book in her hand.

She stood up as I approached, her white face flushing painfully. I noticed that her hair was the same tawny shade as her mother's, but there the likeness ended. She was tall for her age, and extremely thin and frail-looking, with large, intensely blue eyes. She was wearing a very plain and unbecoming dress in a dark grey material.

'Good day. I'm *Fraulein* Burness,' I said cheerfully. Gertrud gave the fire a prod with the long poker and left us together.

'Well,' I continued, 'what do you do all day, now that your governess has left you?'

There was a long silence, during which she seemed to be collecting her wits. 'I try to read Shakespeare in English,' she said.

'And can you understand it?' I saw fear in the blue eyes. She seemed to have lost her tongue completely. I walked over to one of the narrow windows and looked out. The view nearly took my breath away. This part of the schloss rose up stark from the mountainside; below was a terrifying drop. There were window seats, but the windows were barred. I turned round, and for a moment I saw this solitary, subdued child as a prisoner in her own home. I noticed that her nails were bitten to the quick. Compassion for her rose in me so strongly that, although I had already decided not to take the position, I found myself wavering.

'Have you no German books?' I asked.

'Yes, many. But mama said I must read only books written in English now.'

Her mother had made no attempt to speak English to me, and yet she expected this poor child to be fluent in three languages.

'Don't look so afraid,' I said lightly. 'If I do take this position as your governess, I shall want us to be friends.' I smiled at her encouragingly, and to my relief a faint answering smile appeared on her face. I noticed then how delicately chiselled her features were, and how beautiful the large blue eyes. Her skin was fine, but very pale, and her whole appearance was one of extreme fragility. There was nothing robust about this sprig of the von Oldenburg family.

Gradually I drew her out and she began to talk a little about her life in the schoolroom. She had a music teacher, *Frau* Geisner, who came from Goppertal to give her tuition every week. She told me about the cousins who visited her sometimes, who were also von Oldenburgs. In return I told her a little about myself, that like her I was an only child, but an orphan who had been brought up by aunt and uncle. 'My mother was my uncle's sister, so my name is Burness, and his is Nolan,' I explained.

'I have had brothers, though. Three of them,' said Charlotte. 'They all died when they were tiny babies. I remember the last one being born. Mama was ill for a long time afterwards. When you come to live here I will show you our burial ground, and the three little crosses in it. And I'll show you the hollow tree where I used to hide things.'

Before I left the schloss she took me outside for a brief walk. Far below I could see the town of Goppertal, and all around there were mountains. The air was like iced wine.

'The town isn't so far away, really,' said Charlotte. 'When all the church bells are ringing you can hear them echoing round the mountains.'

Without replying I looked at the turrets and the grey grimness of the schloss. The grounds and garden were beautiful, with fountains and statues, but I still hesitated. What would my aunt and uncle think about my taking this position? What would Alistair Harlow think?

'Please come,' begged Charlotte, and I saw tears gathering in her eyes. 'Please come,' she whispered.

'I will give it a trial, Charlotte, if my aunt and uncle are willing. However, if

I don't like it, I can't be expected to stay.'

'But you will like it. I will work very hard at my lessons — ' she broke off, looking down at the cobbled courtyard which was large enough to act as a parade ground for a battalion of infantry, which it doubtless had done in the past. A solitary horseman was just entering the gate. I watched, fascinated by the beauty of the splendid horse, and the air of complete authority which emanated from the rider, even at that distance. A groom hurried forward to take charge of his mount as he swung down from the saddle. Tall, broad-shouldered and narrow-hipped, he walked with a fine, erect carriage towards the great iron-studded door of the castle. How elegant he was, despite his obvious masculinity.

'That's my papa,' said Charlotte, with a mixture of awe and affection in her voice.

I was not to see him again until the day that I officially took up my position as governess to his daughter. Before then I travelled back to England alone and broke the news to Uncle Peter and Aunt Matilda. After talking things over they agreed that I should give it a trial. Uncle Peter had always given me as much freedom as possible, though my aunt had rather more old-fashioned views. However, he usually won her round and it was the same this time, although she dabbed her eyes and said she had hoped to have me home for good after the summer term. I could tell that Alistair Harlow was against the idea, but he was not prepared to risk an argument by saying so. We enjoyed each other's company while I was at home, and took it for granted that we would go on corresponding.

Not long before I left for Germany again I overheard a conversation between my aunt and uncle.

'She's young to be thinking about that sort of thing seriously.'

That was my uncle.

'I'd rather she thought seriously about

that than about some of the things she does. I like Miss Hetherington, but I don't want Marnie to end up like her, a lonely spinster with her head full of books and learning.'

'I doubt that she'll do that, Matilda. But don't start match-making on her behalf, although I agree that young Harlow would make a very acceptable husband. She could go farther and fare worse.'

'She could fare a good deal worse! But there, she's headstrong like her mother was.'

'Yes, and pretty and charming like her, too. The same hazel eyes and wavy brown hair — the same kind, affection-ate nature.'

'A headstrong, affectionate, pretty girl should be married off to a suitable husband as soon as possible. She knows nothing of life outside the schoolroom. She'll find things very different at that castle, or schloss, or whatever it is.'

I crept away.

2

Despite my aunt's misgivings, and Alistair's unspoken disapproval, I took up the position at Schloss Beissel. I felt very nervous on my first day there, when I was summoned to the presence of Count von Oldenburg.

A manservant ushered me into the Count's study and the door was closed behind me. I felt completely overawed. There was a huge writing desk in the room, on which lay very neatly a seal, a crystal letterweight, and an onyx ashtray. There were shotguns on the wall, boars' and stags' heads and a number of photographs of men in military uniform.

'Good day. Please be seated. So you are ... *Fraulein* Burness?' to my surprise, the Count spoke in halting English. I thought it was a charming gesture on his part and some of my nervousness went. His hair was corn-coloured, and seemed to fit his well-shaped head like a helmet. His chin was clean-shaven, a firm chin with a rather engaging cleft in it, and he had a small, military-type moustache. His eyes were the same intense blue as his daughter's and his features were finely chiselled and regular. There was a scar on his cheekbone, a fine, white line running across the clear, healthy skin. It did not detract from his appearance. I judged him to be in his early thirties, which meant that he must have been very young when Charlotte was born.

'I have left the upbringing of my daughter largely in the hands of her mother, with perhaps a word of advice from my own mother, the Dowager Countess,' he explained. 'Her last governess was with her for years — ' He faltered, and then began to speak in German. 'We did not anticipate having to find another one. She speaks French well, but her English is poor. It is our wish that she should speak English all the time with you.'

'I am sorry, Sir, but that will not be possible at first. I shall give priority to her English lessons, but she is very young and it would be unfair to expect too much.'

'Unfair?' He sounded genuinely surprised. 'We expect discipline in the schoolroom.' His fingers drummed restlessly on the desk. His hands were long and slender, and I noticed his right hand was deeply scarred.

'There will be discipline,' I said hastily. 'But I don't think I should put too much pressure on Charlotte at first.' I longed to say that there had been too much discipline in the past; that she was a lonely and nervous child who needed companionship and gaiety in her life.

'H'm.' He stood up and paced the room. Then he seemed to make up his mind. 'Very well, if you think it better that way. It is difficult for me to know what is best for my daughter sometimes. In the case of a son, a military academy solves these problems. That is all, *Fraulein* Burness.'

He was just as arrogant as his wife, I decided, as I left the room. I had no idea of the way back to the schoolroom; I had not dared ask the Count to direct me. The schloss was not as comfortable as I had expected, despite its grandeur. The rooms were enormous, but it was very draughty everywhere, and the plumbing was quite primitive. There was a well out in the courtyard at the back, and every drop of water had to be brought into the schloss from it. The inconvenience and labour which this caused seemed quite ridiculous to me. The *Damenstift* had been very similar, but I had expected more modern ideas altogether at Schloss Beissel. As I walked along thinking this, and trying to find my bearings, a lady came out of a chamber farther up the corridor. She was elderly, very tall and erect, and wearing a beautiful wine-coloured gown with a matching velvet cap on her grey hair. I could tell immediately that she was a person of some importance. She stood and waited for me to walk up to her.

'Good day,' I said. 'I'm afraid I'm lost. I'm the new governess. My name is Marion Burness. I am looking for the way back to the schoolroom.'

'I am Countess Adelaide von Oldenburg,' she said, with pride in every syllable. 'You need not hurry back to the schoolroom. Come into my chamber for a moment.' She led me into a large, splendid room, richly appointed and full of bric-a-brac. A maid was engaged in putting away curling tongs and performing similar duties.

'Be seated.' The Countess indicated a chair covered in crimson plush. I obeyed with some resignation. I was now to be interviewed by the grandmother.

'You are English.' To my surprise she too began to speak in English. It was slow and halting, but her accent was good; far better than her son's. 'One forgets a foreign language so easily. My sister married an Englishman and I stayed with her in London for some time when I was single. Unfortunately, she died in childbirth, and the baby also. To speak English now brings back many memories. My son's tutor taught him English before he went to the military academy, but he is not fluent, although his French is excellent. Countess Maria, his wife, speaks only German.'

She talked of England to me and was interested to hear that my home was on the south coast and that I frequently visited London.

'Charlotte is growing up,' she said. 'There is much that I disapprove of in society today. A child can soon be corrupted. I do not approve of loose ways. The young people accept the Germany of today. I do not. I cannot accept the Prussian ideas — this Bismarck . . . ' she broke off, hatred blazing in her blue eyes.

I remained silent. The swift rise of the new German Reich to world power status evidently had no appeal for the

Dowager Countess. I knew enough of German history to understand and sympathise with her point of view. She wanted the States of southern Germany to remain as they had once been, fiercely independent.

'I believe in self-discipline,' she went on. 'We must fight against this tendency for standards to be lowered.' I realised then that she clung to the idea of frugal living, hard work and a strict moral code. This was in direct contrast to the life led by some of the aristocratic German families, but these high ideals and rigid standards were by no means unknown, even in German royal circles. Hard unremitting work, early rising, adherence to duty, however painful; I had heard that the late Prince Consort had practised these virtues. I listened politely while the Countess expounded on this theme. During a pause I told her that I would do my best for Charlotte.

'I will not detain you any longer, then,' she said, lapsing into German.

Her maid directed me back to the schoolroom.

During that first day with my charge, I discovered a good deal of which I disapproved. The food which Charlotte ate was very plain. She rose at half-past six and breakfasted on rye bread and milk. I had coffee and rolls, which I ate in the schoolroom with her. I was accustomed to German food, but the Countess had sent a message to the kitchen that I could order English dishes if I preferred to. I found that Charlotte was only allowed an egg as a treat, and she was hardly ever allowed cakes and sweetmeats. After the midday meal, *mittagessen*, she had nothing in the afternoon, and only thick milk for supper.

We walked in the grounds together, accompanied by Fritz, one of the many dogs at Schloss Beissel. The warm, dry, south wind, known as the 'snow-eater', had sprung up suddenly, as it often did. A profusion of spring flowers grew everywhere, and birds flew overhead, chirping and singing. Charlotte pointed out an inaccessible spot on the battlements where storks were nesting. Then she took me into an overgrown wilderness of a place, which she told me had been her grandfather's favourite garden. She added that he had died before she was born, but that her grandmother had not allowed anyone to touch it since his death. I could see that the neglected tangle of grass had once been a fine lawn. There was even a fountain, long unused. It was clearly a place with a strong appeal for Charlotte, and it could be made beautiful again. While I was thinking this she gave a sudden cry:

'Papa!'

I looked up and saw the Count watching us from the gate. He was dressed in comfortable-looking tweeds, such as my uncle liked to wear. Fritz, the wolfhound, ran up to him, barking good-naturedly.

'Good day, *Fraulein* Burness. I cannot think what charms this derelict garden holds for you.'

'Good day, Your Excellency,' I said. I took Charlotte's hand in mine. 'I think it could be made into a fine garden, as it once was. Your daughter has told me why it is so neglected. I think it is a great pity.'

'I do not know how my mother, the Countess, feels about it now. I have deferred to her wishes concerning this place. I myself have no objection to it being cultivated again. We have many gardeners. Do you like it here, Charlotte?'

'Oh, yes, Papa.' She flushed with excitement.

'I will mention the matter to your grandmother.' He gave me a keen glance. He probably thought me a bold English Miss, with foreign ideas and no hesitation in expressing them. He was hatless and his hair glinted as bright as a new sovereign in the spring sunshine. He left us abruptly, telling his daughter that he would see her in the drawing room that evening. I watched him walk away and wondered where his wife was. What kind of life did they live in this remote castle? We left the garden by a different way and Charlotte showed me the hollow hawthorn tree where she used to hide things when younger.

Back in the schoolroom, I summoned a maid and ordered coffee and cakes for both of us. Gertrud appeared unexpectedly. Going to a cupboard, she produced a back-board which she proceeded to fasten onto Charlotte, who submitted meekly.

'*Fraulein* Charlotte must wear this until after *mittagessen*,' she said in her guttural voice. 'She wears it every day to correct her carriage.'

As Gertrud was leaving the school-room a maid appeared, bearing a tray with our coffee and cakes. The older woman turned round.

'*Fraulein* Charlotte is not allowed cakes in the morning,' she said, addressing me reprovingly.

'I have permission to order what I require from the kitchen. We have been out walking in the grounds and we are both hungry.'

For a moment Gertrud looked at me without speaking, disbelief on her broad, plain face. 'We will see what the Countess says — we will see,' she muttered finally, and left the room. I had an uneasy feeling that I would hear more about the matter. I asked Charlotte if the back-board was very uncomfortable, but she said she didn't mind it as much as the tight stays she was obliged to wear.

'Mama says I must have a small waist to wear fashionable clothes when I grow up,' she explained dolefully. 'But Gertrud pulls the laces tighter every week.'

'Oh, well, it's all in a good cause, I suppose,' I said lightly, and changed the subject, feeling that I had done enough interfering for one day.

That evening, some time after Charlotte was in bed, I sat in my room writing letters. It was a comfortable room, with a charming boudoir leading off from it.

The bed was soft, with eiderdown and fine linen, and with a bell-rope beside it. The carpet was pale green, and the curtains a soft peach shade. The furniture was of rosewood.

Busy with my letters, I was startled by a knock on the door. I opened it to find a young maidservant there. She told me that the Count and Countess wished to see me. I followed her to the drawing room, wondering uneasily why Charlotte's parents had sent for me. I entered the impressively splendid room, with its candle-lit chandeliers and gilt chairs. The Countess was resting on a *chaise longue*, and the Count was standing in front of the fire, apparently regulating his gold watch. He indicated a chair and I sat down.

'You wished to see me?' I asked, trying to keep the nervousness out of my voice. I looked from one to the other.

The Countess raised her great, amber-coloured eyes and fixed me with a steady stare. 'Yes,' she said. 'Gertrud tells me that you have allowed Charlotte to eat cakes and drink coffee with you this morning. Is this correct?'

'Yes, it is,' I said.

'She is forbidden to eat sweetmeats unless it is a special treat. Gertrud told you this, and yet you still allowed it. Why?'

'Because I was brought up by my uncle, who is a doctor,' I said, deciding to speak my mind, whatever the consequences. 'Charlotte is very tall for her age, and very thin. She rises early and has little breakfast. She has been out walking with me this morning and learning English words. She was ravenously hungry when we came back to the schoolroom. I think she is often in need of extra food.'

The Countess was looking at me in amazement. The Count seemed surprised, but concerned as well. 'Are you suggesting that our daughter is not well fed?' he rapped out, his blue eyes blazing.

'No, not exactly that. But her nails

are badly bitten, and my uncle has a theory that sometimes children bite their nails because their diet is not adequate. I think that Charlotte needs eggs at breakfast and coffee and cakes later in the morning, and — ' My voice faltered and died away under the combined gaze of the Count and Countess.

Charlotte's mother spoke then, her face flushed with anger. 'So! You have only just started here as Charlotte's governess, but already you know better than her parents how to feed her.'

'I did not say that — ' I began, but the Count interrupted me.

'Your uncle has theories about food,' he said. 'Do you consider that you had a better diet as a child than Charlotte?'

'Yes, Your Excellency, I do,' I said boldly. 'I started the day with a good breakfast, which she does not. And I didn't go right from midday to the following morning without a proper meal. She only has thick milk before retiring; it can't be enough for a girl growing as fast as she is. She is five foot four inches now, the same as I am. Tall, thin children can easily go into a decline if they don't get plenty of food.'

'Is that all she has at night — thick milk?' asked the Count, addressing his wife.

'It was enough for me at her age,' she said sullenly.

'You never grew like she's growing.' Her husband seemed about to say more, but controlled himself. I glanced at the Countess' little hands as she nervously twisted them together. A pair of tiny feet encased in patent leather pumps peeped out from under her gown. I realised then that she must be very small; I had never seen her standing.

'The English *fraulein* might be right about this,' he went on. 'I do not care for the idea that Charlotte is sometimes hungry. What did you have to eat before you went to bed as a child, *Fraulein* Burness?'

'I had hot milk and bread spread with beef dripping,' I said, suddenly wanting to laugh. Telling these two aristocrats about my dripping sandwiches seemed ridiculously funny. They, however, saw no humour in it.

The Countess looked sulkily angry, and I could see a glint of annoyance in her husband's eyes, but I had a feeling that he was not annoyed with me.

'In future, Charlotte will be allowed to have more supper,' he told me, ignoring his wife. 'Use your discretion about this matter — see that she has what your uncle would consider a suitable diet for a tall girl of her age.'

'Thank you, Your Excellency,' I said.

'I shall inspect her nails in about a month's time,' said his wife tartly.

'I will not have Charlotte going to bed hungry.' The Count spoke firmly, and I noticed that he had flushed slightly, so that the livid scar on his cheekbone showed more. He changed the subject. 'Concerning the other matter, Charlotte's grandmother has consented to allow the garden to be cultivated again. She has no objection if you and Charlotte use it.'

'Thank you. How splendid!' I exclaimed impulsively. 'May I ask the gardeners to start digging the soil over?'

'I see no reason why not.' The Countess said nothing. There was a look of baffled anger on her face, and I left the room feeling both elated and slightly uneasy.

★ ★ ★

'I have a daughter about your age,' said *Frau* Geisner, rapidly sorting through some sheets of music. 'You must come and visit us in Goppertal. I have twin girls of twelve also. We would be pleased to see you any time.'

Frau Geisner smiled her wide, engaging smile as Charlotte sat at the piano. She was fat and jolly, with keen, dark eyes and black corkscrew curls framing her plump face. I soon found out that besides being an accomplished musician, she was also a quite shameless gossip. Out of earshot of her young pupil, she began to talk about the von Oldenburgs.

'They're eaten up with pride, but I expect you've noticed that. That brother who was killed — Otto — he was a terrible rake. Gambling, women, drink, just about everything you can think of. And then, when all the arrangements had been made for his wedding, he got killed in a gaming duel.'

'A duel! I didn't know they still had them.'

'Perhaps not, officially. The man who killed him fled the country.'

'How terrible for the von Oldenburg family,' I said. 'And for the bride-to-be.'

'Yes, but the present Count Carl, his younger brother who was on active service with the army, came home on leave and married her instead.'

'The present Countess?'

'Yes. She was sixteen, no more. And he was only nineteen. Then he was wounded and taken prisoner, but not for long. He came out of the army with the Iron Cross and a wounded hand.'

'Yes, Charlotte told me that.'

'It's my belief he still hankers after the army. He's not like his brother, but that young cousin of his, Georg, he's just like him. They have to watch their daughters in Goppertal when he comes to stay. Countess Maria is selfish and idle, and she won't bear again, they say. Three dead sons in a row — ah, the torchlight processions in Goppertal after each one! All the church bells ringing, but they rejoiced too soon. The old Countess is a fine woman. She still goes to visit the poor and she did much for the wounded during the war.'

The Franco-Prussian war was still talked about in these parts, although it was now more than a decade since it had ended. But I had seen the pride of the army officers in Leiknar; Count von Oldenburg had the same arrogant bearing. They could not forget their victory, any more than the French could forget the humiliation of their defeat.

'As for that poor little thing — ' *Frau*

Geisner jerked her head in the direction of Charlotte — 'my twins have a better life than she does. That sour old *Fraulein* Schiller made things miserable for her. But she looks happier now you are her governess.'

I had no intention of becoming a prisoner in the schloss, and the following Sunday morning I decided to take advantage of *Frau* Geisner's invitation. I set out to walk down the mountain road to Goppertal. It was a delightful mediaeval town. Some of the houses had beautiful wood carvings on the outside, and the shops had gold-painted signs on the eaves. There were no pavements, so pedestrians had to be ever alert, as coachmen drove through with loud cries of 'Ho! Ho!' Its three churches were all beautiful; one had a spire that rose loftily far above the buildings below; a monument built in the twelfth century, to the glory of God.

I knew that mists were a common occurrence in these parts, but I was not prepared for one quite as thick as the one I walked into not far from the schloss. It swirled around me, damply chill, and so dense that I could not see more than a couple of yards ahead. I heard the sound of horses' hooves and drew to one side for safety. Out of the thick whiteness horse and rider appeared, and I recognised the Count.

'*Fraulein* Burness! What are you doing on the mountain road in this mist?'

'I am walking into the town, Your Excellency.'

'It is not necessary! Arrangements can be made — '

'Thank you, but I enjoy walking.'

'But harm could come to you.'

'I am not afraid.'

He began to speak in halting English. 'That does not matter. I am — er — responsible for your safety while you are under my roof. If harm came to you, what would your uncle think? That good doctor who had you so well . . . so well-feeded as a child.'

I burst out laughing. 'All those wasted dripping sandwiches,' I said.

The Count was not amused. 'I was not making a joke,' he said in German. He swung down from his black horse and stood beside me. As he did so, I heard the sound of church bells in the town.

'Listen,' he said. 'You will hear the echo.'

A few moments later it seemed as if the mountains themselves were full of bells. The sound of them ringing rolled backwards and forwards and I stood enchanted. Then the mist began to clear. The sun broke through and lit the scene with splendour. A vista of pine trees and flowers, mountains and valleys rose up before us, with the climbing brown roofs of little hamlets far below. Suddenly it all seemed unreal, like a fairy-tale, and this Count standing beside me was part of it.

'*Das ist der Tag des Herren*,' he said softly.

I had heard those words 'This is the Lord's day' on *Frau* Krafft's lips sometimes on a Sunday. He turned from the view below and faced me.

'As the mist is lifting, it should be safe for you to walk down to the town now. But I must warn you that there are some rough and unruly peasants living in these parts. Some of your English ideas will be of no use here, *Fraulein* Burness. Remember, it is not England.'

He remounted and gave me a slight nod of farewell before riding off in the direction of the schloss. I enjoyed my day in Goppertal at *Frau* Geisner's house. It was a solid, delightful, untidy dwelling place overlooking the river. I met her big, jolly schoolmaster husband and the flaxen-haired twins, also her nineteen-year-old daughter, Emma, who was very friendly and charming.

That night I sat at the rosewood bureau in my room, writing letters home. I was just beginning to find my way around at the schloss, and I was intrigued to find that from my window I could actually see the hollow hawthorn tree outside the forbidden garden. But it was not forbidden any longer . . .

A knock on the door made me start. I opened it to find Heinrich, the Count's valet standing there. '*Fraulein*!' He clicked his heels smartly. Charlotte had told me that he had been the Count's orderly during the war, and had served him as a civilian ever since. 'The Count asked me to see if you had returned safely.'

'Thank you. As you see, I am back.'

'Very well, *fraulein*.' He bade me goodnight and was gone. I retired, although sleep was long in coming. My window was open and as I lay there in the silence I thought I heard footsteps outside. Overcome with sudden curiosity, I got out of bed and looked down through the window. In the moonlight I could see a man walking alone on the cobblestones. I recognised the figure of Count von Oldenburg.

The following morning the Countess sent for me not long before *mittagessen*. The same feeling of annoyance rose in me as when she had first interviewed me, straight from her tumbled bed. Gertrud was lacing her into some new stays and for a few moments the Countess scarcely glanced at me, she was so busy admiring herself in the mirror. The tiny circumference of whalebone-girdled waist grew smaller and smaller, until the Countess declared that it was tight enough. Then she turned her attention to me, sitting down without a trace of self-consciousness, although half-undressed, with her tawny hair hanging loose to her waist.

She told me that there would be visitors in the schloss for a few weeks, and that Charlotte's cousin Frederica would be there. She asked me if I would be willing to have Frederica in the schoolroom with Charlotte, adding that, naturally, I would receive extra pay for this service.

'Certainly. The company of another girl will be good for Charlotte,' I said.

The Countess seemed pleased. Indeed, her manner was extremely amiable, and she appeared to be looking forward to the expected guests. Our brief business concluded, she dismissed me with a wave of her little hand and told Gertrud that she was ready to try on her new ball gown. I withdrew, irritated that she did not trouble to be dressed when she received me. The smell of her scent was still in my nostrils. She seemed such a shallow creature, and yet she had enchanted both the von Oldenburg brothers . . .

'Wait until Frederica sees the garden,' said Charlotte excitedly that afternoon. She was eagerly anticipating her cousins' visit.

'Now, repeat that in English,' I said. We were both in the garden, pulling and hacking at weeds, while two men were busy digging it over and levelling it. We had an unexpected visitor in the shape of the Dowager Countess.

She stood watching us for a few minutes. 'So many years, *Fraulein* Burness,' she said, speaking in her careful English. 'So many years since anyone touched this place. My husband tended it himself. He loved it. We used to sit in it together.'

'We must make it so that you can sit in it again, Your Excellency,' I said cheerfully. I noticed then how drawn and ill she looked. 'Are you feeling quite well?' I asked, thinking that perhaps I was impertinent to ask such a personal question.

'I often feel unwell,' she replied. 'I shall be seeing a specialist soon.'

'I hope, then, that it is a passing indisposition,' I said.

She smiled, but there seemed to be something bitter and resigned about that smile.

'I hope, too, that you will be well enough to enjoy the company of your guests,' I continued.

'Yes. They are my late husband's cousin and his family. Five sons and one girl, Frederica.'

'Countess Maria seems to be looking forward to their visit.'

'No doubt.' The other woman's lips tightened as she spoke. 'Charlotte is looking much brighter these days,' she said, changing the subject. 'You appear to be a good influence, *Fraulein* Burness.'

'Thank you,' I said. I called Charlotte away from her weeding to speak to her grandmother for a few minutes. Then the Countess Adelaide left us, walking away in her slow, dignified manner.

It was true that Charlotte was looking much better. She rarely bit her nails during the day, and I had persuaded her to wear cotton gloves at night. The daily gardening sharpened her appetite, which was now satisfied by an ample and varied diet, and the fresh air whipped colour into her pale cheeks. We also rode in the grounds together, talking in a mixture of English, French and German. I had not thought that being a governess would be so tiring, but I found myself quite exhausted by night time, particularly during the first few weeks.

3

'See, *Fraulein* Burness, how I am helping you,' said Georg von Oldenburg, showing his white teeth in a smile. He bent down and pulled up a clump of weeds. 'We all know how strange the English are, how eccentric. Young English ladies can be very charming, though.'

I smiled politely, as I continued with my weeding. Charlotte and Frederica were both helping me. Her brothers seemed to be swarming everywhere; how the schloss had changed during the past three weeks. It had not changed for the worse, though. It had just become extremely noisy. And everyone seemed too busy with other matters to bother about whether Charlotte was getting enough discipline or not. I rather think the same applied to her fair-haired cousin, Frederica. However, she coped quite well in the schoolroom, but certainly lessons were cut down, and more and more of my time was spent supervising the girls in outdoor activities. There were a good many of these. Riding and driving out for picnics was a favourite pastime, both with the adults and the children.

The men went fishing a good deal; Count von Oldenburg, his cousin once removed, Charles, and Charles' son, Georg. There was another man with the von Oldenburg party, too, a relative of theirs, a man of about thirty-five, Baron Gustav von Schilsky. He was strikingly handsome; dark, completely different from the von Oldenburgs in appearance. Frederica's four other brothers, aged between sixteen and twenty-two, were also keen fishermen, although the youngest, Hadrach, sometimes helped us in the garden.

It did not take me long to realise that Georg von Oldenburg was interested in me. This did not altogether surprise me, after what *Frau* Geisner and her husband had told me about him. I avoided him as much as possible.

Other guests had come to stay at the schloss, and, far from being the quiet place which I had once thought it, it now buzzed with activity. The enormous number of servants at Schloss Beissel was now swelled by the servants of visiting families. The summer was racing by; apple blossom time was just a memory now; indeed, they were busy harvesting the rye. The sun shone every day; the heat was quite oppressive sometimes, even situated high up as we were. Down in the town the baking cobblestones were warm to the feet. The old trees by the Town Hall drooped, their brown leaves thick with dust. The familiar smell of roasting coffee which haunted most houses and stairways was intensified, as was the smell of household refuse.

Every three or four days sudden storms swept up, tropical in their violence. Blasts of thunder cracked like splitting beams; lightning zigzagged round the mountains; rain fell in white, sizzling sheets. But the morning after, it was as hot as ever. Work in the garden went steadily ahead. I rarely saw the Dowager Countess now. She kept to her own rooms most of the time. She did, however, emerge when the von Oldenburgs gave a ball.

They gave a ball every summer, to celebrate a local legend. This particular piece of folklore had happened so long ago that its origins were lost in speculation. One year there was supposed to have been a very bad drought in the neighbourhood, and the people prayed for rain. A strange but beautiful woman was said to have appeared on the mountainside. She had a long wand in her hand, and, waving it on high, she caused rain to fall for many days. A young man fell in love with her, but when he tried to come close to her, she ran away. He pursued her to the edge of a dangerous precipice, whereupon she turned into a bird of exquisite plumage and flew away. The young man fell to his death far below, and that was how the legend of the Rain Bird began. This myth accounted for the rather strange-looking bird which was so prominently featured on the von Oldenburg crest.

The people of Goppertal had turned this rather fanciful story into a summer festival and the von Oldenburgs joined in with their own celebrations. The castle was decorated with garlands of flowers, and a sumptuous banquet was being prepared in the kitchens.

The day before the ball, Count von Oldenburg appeared unexpectedly in the schoolroom. 'You are attending our ball tomorrow, *Fraulein* Burness?' he said, half as a question, half as a statement. Charlotte and Frederica had already told me that they were going to be allowed to attend it, and that, naturally, I would be expected to. I said that I would wait until I was invited. I had a feeling that my words had been repeated to the von Oldenburgs.

'If I am expected to,' I replied demurely.

'You are most certainly expected to. It is a summer festival here. Even though you are English, you will enjoy it. I hope so — ' he suddenly broke off, but not before I had seen in his eyes that he really wanted me to go. 'I would like you to enjoy yourself,' he finished quietly.

'Thank you, Your Excellency,' I said. 'I am sure I shall do that.'

'You must be very busy just now, with Frederica to instruct as well as Charlotte. I hope you are not finding it too much for you.'

'Not at all. The girls keep each other company. Indeed, in many ways it is easier having two pupils.'

'They will both be at the ball tomorrow, as you know. But they are not to stay up to the end, as it will be very late.' He left the schoolroom then, and the three of us fell to discussing the forthcoming ball. A group of musicians had been engaged to play for us, and both the girls were excited at being allowed to attend.

The following day dawned fine and warm again, and there was a holiday atmosphere everywhere. Between Gertrud and myself there existed a kind of armed neutrality. She had not forgotten that I had got my own way concerning Charlotte's diet, and in one or two other matters, and she made it plain that she disapproved and that I had better not try to change the established order of things too much. She had expertly altered a ball gown which the Countess no longer wore into a charming dress for Charlotte, and she was about to give it a final ironing. Rather to my surprise, she asked gruffly if mine needed ironing as well, and offered to do it. As she was far more competent than any of the laundry maids, I took advantage of her offer. My ball gown had been a gift from my aunt for my eighteenth birthday, and it was of cream-coloured watered taffeta, flounced, but otherwise quite plain. It was beautifully styled, though, and I did not feel I need be ashamed of it, even at the von Oldenburgs' ball.

I felt in quite high spirits preparing for the festivities that evening. By this time I had grown accustomed to the lack of plumbing, and also to the indifference towards such matters at the schloss. Having a hip-bath in a few inches of cool water was a normal procedure to me now. I piled my hair high on my head and wore the garnet earrings and necklace which had been my mother's. The *Rittersaal*, the hall of the knights, was where the ball was being held. It was a beautiful chamber with an exquisitely-carved lime-wood ceiling, and portraits of long-dead von Oldenburgs lining the walls. It was bedecked with greenery now, and chains of edelweiss, gentians and other wild flowers were everywhere. The musicians were assembled ready to play, and the ball officially began when the Count took his wife's hand and led her onto the floor to start the dancing with a cotillion.

Countess Maria was in a gown of

pale green, which set off her unusual colouring to perfection. How tiny she was, I thought. Her head scarcely reached her husband's shoulder. Then, rather to my surprise, several gentlemen approached me and asked if they might book dances. There was much heel-clicking and bowing from the waist. Georg von Oldenburg pushed his way forward and announced that he had already booked the next dance with me. The other men politely deferred to him and I found myself swept out onto the floor in his arms. It was a fast German waltz. He squeezed my hand and smiled down at me.

'Now I know what an English rose really looks like, *Fraulein* Burness. No longer the busy little schoolmarm; with your hair beautifully arranged and wearing a delightful gown, you blossom out as a great beauty. Why have you come to Germany and to my cousin's schloss? Perhaps you are pursued by some ardent suitor and you do not want him.'

'You are extremely fanciful,' I said, smiling. 'Nothing as romantic as that, I can assure you. I am sure your cousin Charlotte has told you that I have been to school in Germany and that I took this position to gain experience. I might become a school teacher.'

'What an ambition for a beautiful girl like yourself.'

'I see nothing wrong with it.' I spoke coolly.

'You do not wish to be a wife?'

'I might be, some day. But I do not intend to rush into marriage — ' I broke off as I had been on the point of saying 'with the first man who asks me'. I was uncomfortably reminded of my uncle's words concerning Alistair — 'She could go farther, and fare worse'.

'*Ach*, so you have some modern ideas — foreign ways, I suppose.'

'I certainly don't agree with the idea that girls should be expected to get married as soon as possible.'

'And I suppose arranged marriages strike you as being quite wrong?'

'Quite wrong,' I said firmly. He inclined his blonde head and appeared to be considering this remark. He was a shorter, stockier build than the Count, but quite good-looking, although a trifle florid in the face.

'Tell me, *Fraulein* Burness, what do you think of Charlotte?'

'Charlotte? I think she is a sweet child, and very intelligent.'

'And what sort of woman do you think she will become?'

'I think she will become a very elegant and cultured woman. She should also be warm and affectionate. That is, if — ' I paused, remembering that he was a von Oldenburg.

'If what?'

'If she is not too strictly dealt with.'

'So you think her upbringing has been harsh?'

'I did not say that.'

'But it is true that you have made certain changes in the schoolroom since you came here.'

'I have made one or two changes,

with the permission of her parents.'

'So I understand.'

'I am surprised, Sir, that you take such an interest in your young cousin's upbringing.'

'Are you indeed?' He smiled and guided me along. He had booked several dances, but was obliged to give me up to another young man for the next.

I noticed Baron von Schilsky dancing with Countess Maria. How intently they were looking at each other, I thought. Then the Count himself claimed his dance with me and we moved onto the floor.

'You are enjoying it, *Fraulein* Burness?'

'It is delightful,' I said. 'The music is enchanting, and the flowers are lovely. It's rather warm for dancing, but I keep fanning myself when the music stops. Charlotte and Frederica are having a wonderful time, too.'

'Splendid,' he said gravely, hissing the 's', his face solemn as it always was when he spoke in English. I felt somewhat awed dancing with him. He danced superbly; I could feel the muscular hardness of his shoulder under my hand as we waltzed.

'You must not be shocked if you see some of the guests imbibing fairly freely later on,' he continued, speaking in German now. 'Charlotte and her cousin will be in bed by then. I am afraid we tend to over-eat, and perhaps drink a little too much at the Festival of the Rain Bird. Also, there is a ceremony enacted during the evening, in which the young unmarried men put the names of the young ladies on scraps of paper, and someone draws a name out of a hat and that girl is the Rain Bird. Then the ladies do the same with the names of the single men. The girl has to run away then, and she is pursued and kissed by the young man. It is all . . . what do you say in English?'

'Fun?' I suggested.

'Yes. So you will not be alarmed?'

'No, of course not,' I said. 'I shall

look forward to it.'

Count von Oldenburg was right about the drinking. The banquet was indeed lavish. I had never seen so much food in my life, and champagne, Mosel wine, and beer flowed freely. The heat, combined with the smell of flowers, was almost overpowering. White-gloved footmen, powdered and bewigged, were serving, and I realised with a sense of shock that some of them were not too steady on their feet as the hour grew later. The musicians played more and more wildly as they reached for their glasses of wine, which were constantly replenished. The noise and confusion reached a peak when lots were drawn for the Rain Bird.

I had not expected my name to be included, and I felt myself flushing when I heard it read out from the chosen slip of paper. The next moment the Count was in front of me, smiling and bowing with a great show of courtesy.

'*Fraulein* Burness! Congratulations

— you are the Rain Bird. Please come forward.' He took my hand and led me into the centre of the floor. 'This is the Rain Bird. *Fraulein* Burness, from England.'

There was much good-natured applause and cries of '*Der Regenvogel! Der Regenvogel!*'

'It sounds prettier in English,' I said nervously.

'You make a charming Rain Bird,' said the Count's mother, who, although she did not look well, was elegantly dressed in a gown of grey silk. She gave me a kind, warm smile. Minutes afterwards the name of the young man was announced. It was Georg von Oldenburg. I had a feeling that somehow he had managed to arrange this.

'Now you had better fly,' said Countess Maria, languidly wafting herself with an exquisite ivory fan. 'Run where you wish, and hide, so that he cannot find you.'

Urged on by the rest of the company,

I hurried from the hall and up the stairs. I did not want to spoil the fun of the evening, but I was not very pleased at being the Rain Bird. After hours of dancing the effort of running upstairs in that tight-waisted, billowing dress made my heart pound. I was thankful I had only drunk two glasses of wine. As I stood hesitating, wondering which way to go, there was a great hubbub from down below and I saw Georg von Oldenburg tearing up the stairs after me, cheered on by a noisy crowd. I was suddenly panic-stricken. Taking to my heels, I ran as fast as I could despite the hampering dress I was wearing. It no longer seemed as if we were acting out a pretty legend; Georg's face was flushed with drink and his eyes were glinting with the thrill of the hunt.

Where should I go? I flew along the nearest corridor. Should I dash into one of the rooms — any room? I tried a door. It was locked, and that slowed me up. Georg was rapidly gaining on me now; I dare not try another door.

The next moment he caught hold of me and I screamed in spite of myself.

'What is wrong, my pretty, pretty Rain Bird?' His arms were round me, holding me so tightly that I could not move; could scarcely breathe. His mouth pressed down on mine, raining kiss after kiss on me. 'And so very clever of you to run in this direction,' he murmured. 'So very clever of you, my sweet English Rain Bird.'

'Let me go!' I gasped, as soon as I could speak. 'You've caught me and kissed me, so we can go back to the hall now.'

'No, not so fast,' he said, pulling me along the corridor. 'My room is not so far away — yes, here we are.' Holding my arm with one hand, he opened a door and pushed me into the room in front of him. Fear such as I had never experienced before rose in me.

I knew how thick all the castle walls were, that if I screamed nobody would hear. It was dusk, but not yet dark.

'Let me go!' I cried. 'You can't keep

me here — ' My voice rose to a scream as he dragged me over to the bed.

'Be quiet,' he said roughly, pushing me down. 'What do you expect?'

He quickly turned the key in the door. Already I had sprung up from the bed, but he dragged me back and pushed me down again. This was no game, I knew, but it was unspeakable, disgusting that he should behave like this. He hurriedly began to remove his jacket, but he had scarcely done so when there was a loud banging on the door.

'Georg! Open this door, please.' It was the Count's voice. In a flash Georg slipped his jacket on again, ran his fingers through his hair and unlocked the door.

'Yes, Carl?' he said, smiling innocently. The Count stepped into the room, obviously taking in my dishevelled appearance.

'Well,' he said, 'evidently you have been caught and kissed, *Fraulein* Burness. You dropped your fan outside the door.' He handed it to me. 'Come now, back to the dancing. You have been . . . what do you say in English?'

'A good sport,' I suggested, glancing coldly at Georg.

'A *gut* sport,' repeated the Count, making the phrase sound peculiar. He shepherded me back along the corridors and down the stairs. My heart was still thumping with fear. Georg trailed rather sullenly behind us. I was under no illusions as to what would have happened if the Count had not come along when he did. I had a strong suspicion that he was under no illusions either. When we arrived back in the candle-lit brightness of the *Rittersaal*, I could see that his eyes were hard, although he was smiling.

I sat down and fanned myself vigorously. Georg did not claim his next dance with me. I had a feeling that either he was too ashamed of his behaviour or else he was sulking. In any case it was high time that Charlotte and Frederica were in bed. I took them away before their parents could complain that they were up too late. They were both tired, but wide-eyed and excited, and they were very intrigued because I had been picked as the Rain Bird.

I returned to the ball. By now, though, it was no longer very well organised. Some of the musicians were clearly the worse for drink — *weinfroh* was what the Germans called it. The dancing went on in fits and starts; the footmen continued to serve drink, but there was no concealing the fact that by now most of them were appallingly drunk themselves.

I knew that the festivities went on until nearly dawn, but I had no intention of staying up to the end. I had no lack of dancing partners, and most of the gentlemen paid me elaborate compliments. Officially, being the Rain Bird, I was what we would call the belle of the ball in England. Georg did not pay me any further attentions, however, for which I was grateful. The darkly handsome Gustav von Schilsky did not book a dance with me, but Charles von Oldenburg, Georg's father, danced a polka with me in a rather wild fashion. It was plain to see that he was *weinfroh*. At one point he almost stumbled, which alarmed me, as he would certainly have brought me crashing down with him. After that experience I decided to retire and slipped away quietly to my room.

As I undressed and prepared for bed I pondered on the events of the evening, and how badly Georg von Oldenburg had behaved. *Frau* Geisner had told me that a lot of the young people in Goppertal went a bit wild on the night of the Rain Bird festival. She assured me that a number of spring babies were born as a result of it, and I was quite prepared to believe her. It was a relief when I was finally out of all constricting garments and sitting in front of the dressing-table in my nightgown. I did not linger long with my toilet, but slipped into bed after unpinning my hair. I had barely done so before I heard the faint sound of voices and footsteps below the window. Curiosity made me get out of bed and investigate, as I had done once before. Was it the Count again, walking round the schloss as he sometimes did, I wondered. The moonlight was quite bright and I could make out two figures, closely entwined. I saw the gleam of a pale dress in the silvery light, and recognised Countess Maria. Then I realised with a stab of surprise that the man she was with was not the Count. As I watched, I saw him bend and kiss her. Then they walked on slowly, still entwined. I caught my breath with shock and disgust. Feeling quite stunned, I climbed back into bed. I lay staring at the chink of moonlight shining through a gap in the curtains, where I had not drawn them carefully enough. So this was what went on in Schloss Beissel, behind the proud veneer of the von Oldenburgs. Who was the man who had been with the Countess? From the fleeting glimpse which I had caught of him, I suspected that he was von Schilsky. He had danced with the Countess several times . . .

And the Count — what of him? Was he enjoying himself in the company of another woman? No, I thought not. The Count was above such cheap behaviour, I was sure of that. Nor did I think that he would countenance it in others. He had hurried after Georg because he was afraid of what might happen to me. It was fortunate indeed that I had dropped my fan outside the door of Georg's room.

I felt strangely disturbed lying there. The Count was so proud. I was sure that he would be enraged at his wife daring to sneak off into the grounds of the castle like a serving wench, and allow another man to embrace her. As for his mother, what would she think? I had a feeling that she had no high opinion of her daughter-in-law as it was . . .

Georg von Oldenburg was a rake, there was no doubt about that. If he wanted a girl, he saw no reason why he should not have her. How dare he think I was available for his pleasure? At last I fell asleep from sheer exhaustion.

The following day everyone seemed rather tired, not surprisingly. I heard that Countess Adelaide, the Count's mother, had been ill in the night and that the house-party was breaking up sooner than planned. Whether this had anything to do with the Dowager Countess' illness I was not sure. It was rather an anti-climax after all the preparations for the ball. Frederica was sorry to go, but said she would be back in the autumn, when the hunting season began. They came from Wotan, a town of about ten miles east of Goppertal.

Georg came into the schoolroom before they departed. 'I will say a special goodbye now,' he said, addressing Charlotte. 'Later you will be waving me off. Work hard at your lessons and be an obedient girl.'

Rather to my surprise he took Charlotte in his arms and kissed her, not with a cousinly kiss but with a curious sort of restrained passion. Watching him I felt uneasy. She was a mere child, not yet fourteen. I caught his whispered '*Liebling*' before he released her. Then he turned to me, his face impudent.

'And now I will kiss your governess — the Rain Bird — goodbye.'

I longed to say that it was not necessary, but I did not like to make a fuss in front of Charlotte. He seized me and kissed me in much the same way as he had his young cousin. We watched him go out of the schoolroom.

'Are you coming to wave them all goodbye when they go?' asked Charlotte.

'Well, I'm not one of the family, Charlotte,' I said gently. 'I do not think that it is my place to do that.'

A few days after the guests had departed, Countess Maria sent for me. She informed me that she and the Count and Charlotte would be visiting her family in Karismette, a town situated several miles north of Goppertal. She added that, as Countess Adelaide was not very well they would like me to act as a companion to her while they were absent.

'Is that agreeable to you?' she asked.

'Yes . . . I think so,' I said slowly. 'If she should have need for a doctor, would she tell me so?' I felt that I did not want to have the responsibility of a sick woman, and it seemed as if the von Oldenburgs were expecting that of me. Although it was approaching midday, as usual at that hour Countess Maria was in her *peignoir*, her hair a tawny tangle down her back. Although she was about ten years older than me and had a daughter of thirteen, looking at her with her small oval face and curiously inviting, voluptuous little body, I felt that in many ways she was a child. A beautiful, wayward child who had somehow come to live at Schloss Beissel, where she did not belong.

I knew that her husband would have

been up for hours, probably out dealing with the affairs of his estate. And his mother, despite her ill-health, would never receive anyone unless she was properly dressed. Gertrud lumbered around, putting clothes to rights and preparing for her mistress to make a leisurely toilet. For some time now I had been in the habit of loosening Charlotte's stays during the daytime, so she had been much more comfortable and Gertrud was none the wiser.

While I was talking to the Countess her husband appeared in the room. He looked surprised when he saw me, but greeted me courteously.

'You are not ill, Maria?' He looked pointedly at his wife's *déshabillé*

'No, I am asking *Fraulein* Burness if she will attend to your mother while we are away,' she replied coolly.

'She does not have to attend to her,' he said sharply. 'If you will be good enough to give the Countess a little companionship every day,' he went on, addressing me, 'we shall be grateful.'

The Count, as usual, was immaculately turned out; it was plain that his wife's slovenliness displeased him. I could not help thinking that without a maid to attend to her she would be in a sorry plight.

'I think that is all. You may leave us now, *Fraulein* Burness,' he said a little curtly. I left the room thinking about this new task which had been thrust on me.

4

The expected thing, really, would have been for me to accompany my young charge on any visits. Evidently the von Oldenburgs had decided that the Dowager Countess needed me more than did Charlotte while they were away. What a strange man the Count was, I thought. Although he had joined in the spirit of the merrymaking the night of the ball, I did not think that he was a very happy man. Why had he married his brother's bride-to-be?

I thought of the von Oldenburgs' burial ground. Charlotte had taken me there one day and shown me the three little white crosses which marked the graves of her baby brothers. Three dead sons and a wife who flirted with other men. Did he know about her? I pondered on this as I taught Charlotte that day. There was a noticeable improvement in his daughter in every way. By making a tremendous effort, Charlotte had controlled her nail-biting and, at long last, pretty oval nails were beginning to grow, much to her delight. The gardening and the long walks which we took every day had brought a faint, becoming pink into her once-pale cheeks and she was looking less frail.

As much as I dared, I had eased the discipline which *Fraulein* Schiller had imposed upon her and she was less nervous as a result. And certainly the company of Frederica had done her a great deal of good. I fell to thinking of Frederica's brother, Georg. I had not cared for the way he had kissed Charlotte. It was one thing for him to embrace me with passion, but quite another for him to kiss his little cousin like that. He had never apologised to me for his conduct on the night of the ball and, having rescued me from that unpleasant predicament, the Count had not mentioned it again. It seemed that such lapses of behaviour were ignored at Schloss Beissel. Other matters were discussed freely, though. The changes which I had made in the schoolroom were apparently known to Georg. But what business of his was the upbringing of Charlotte, a cousin several times removed? In my letters to my aunt and uncle, and to Alistair, I usually referred to my life at the schloss as interesting. It was undoubtedly that, but there were a number of things which I didn't care for.

I bade Charlotte an affectionate farewell as she set off on her journey with her parents. The splendid black carriage bearing the von Oldenburg crest, the green-liveried coachmen and outriders made an impressive sight, with a retinue of servants in other carriages. So this was how the family travelled to Charlotte's grandparents in Karismette. The Dowager Countess smiled at me after they had gone.

'We shall have the castle to ourselves now, Miss Burness,' she said in her careful, correct English. 'Bring your embroidery, or whatever you have, crochet work, perhaps, to my room in the mornings — and evenings too, if you wish. I shall sleep in the afternoons. I find it difficult to sleep at night.'

'I am sorry about that.'

'My days are numbered,' she said quietly. For a moment her remark left me nonplussed.

'Surely not, Your Excellency . . . ' I murmured, and felt again a curious, inexplicable sympathy with this woman, although I disagreed with so many of her ideas.

'Do not pity me. I shall go on leading a normal life for as long as I can. The tragedy of life is not that one dies, but that one dies and leaves uncompleted tasks behind. If I could perhaps live another two years I could see Charlotte married.'

'Charlotte married? Why, in two years' time she will be barely sixteen — she is not yet fourteen.'

The Countess nodded. 'She will mature a great deal over the next two years, I have no doubt.'

As she had suggested, I brought the shawl which I was crocheting and spent the following morning in her company. I planned to ride in the afternoon and perhaps spend some time with her in the evening. She had her own apartments in the schloss, and her sitting room was well appointed and full of flowers. There were many silver-framed photographs in the room, including one of the Count in the uniform of an officer. How very young he looked, I thought, and how handsome. There was also a photograph of another young man. Something in the cast of his features reminded me of Georg von Oldenburg. The Countess, who was sitting rigidly straight in a high-backed chair embroidered with the Oldenburg emblem, noticed that I was looking at it.

'That was my other son, Otto,' she said. 'It was a great tragedy that he died the way he did. I shall never get over it, never.'

I was surprised that she had mentioned it to me, still more that she had told me how deeply it had affected her.

'I had heard of it,' I said. 'It was fortunate that you were spared your other son, Your Excellency.'

'Fortunate indeed — and he a soldier: just a badly-scarred hand to show for it and not the full use of his fourth finger. But I had hoped for grandsons, and it is not to be. I doubt if I shall live to see Charlotte's children.' Having said that she appeared to dismiss the matter and talked of other things. She asked me about my home life in England.

'You do not intend to get married, then?'

'Certainly not for some time yet. I think a girl should see something of life before settling down.'

'It depends on the girl. I myself travelled and had an interesting time before I married. But then, I was a girl who could take care of myself. I was always chaperoned, of course, although it was not really necessary with me. I was very level-headed. In fact, I was something like yourself, I think. When you were chosen to be the Rain Bird, you took it very calmly. I expected that you would join in the merry-making without being foolish or losing your dignity, and you did. You and Georg were soon seen in the *Rittersaal* again.'

Thanks to her son, I thought, but said nothing.

'Georg reminds me very much of Otto,' she went on. 'Otto had much love of gaiety. He loved dancing and hunting — and gambling, I am sorry to say . . . ' she broke off with a wistful little shake of her head. She had not said that her dead son loved women; it probably went without saying. She seemed kindly disposed towards Georg, though. Did she know anything about the other side of him, I wondered. The unpleasant side, which could allow him to drag an unwilling girl into his room with one intention in mind? But no, how could she?

'He seems very fond of Charlotte,' I said. 'He takes an interest in what she is doing in the schoolroom.'

The Countess nodded approvingly. 'Georg will be ready to settle down and get married in a couple of years,' she said. 'And by that time Charlotte will be ready for marriage, too.'

'She will have to meet some suitable young men first,' I said, not wishing to show my disapproval too much.

'That will not be necessary with a husband already found for her.'

I was about to say, 'What husband?', but suddenly I realised the implication behind her remarks. Charlotte was to marry Georg von Oldenburg! Why, it was disgusting; unthinkable. I thought with anger of the harsh discipline which had been imposed upon the girl throughout her childhood, and her childhood would barely be over before she became her cousin's wife. It was outrageous; nor could I see any reason for it. I was sure she knew nothing of this plan.

'Does Charlotte know that Georg is

to be her husband?' I asked, hiding my feeling as best I could and speaking casually.

'Not yet, but I believe her parents will tell her when she is fourteen. She will have plenty of time to get used to the idea. Georg has known for some time, of course.'

No wonder he took such an interest in her progress, I thought. And that kiss which he had given her — he had merely been tasting what was to be his completely in two years or so. And the poor child knew nothing of it yet. Oh, it was unspeakable!

'Well, I shall certainly not mention it,' I said. 'I know that in Germany many things are different, but it seems rather unfair — '

The Countess bridled at that remark. 'There is no question of it being fair or unfair,' she said, and her voice was firm. 'It is Charlotte's duty to marry Georg. It is her duty to her father — to the von Oldenburgs. If she did not marry Georg, what would become of the

Oldenburg name? It will die out in this branch of the family unless she marries Georg. If she marries him there will be no complications. Her name will remain the same and eventually the schloss will be theirs. I hope that Charlotte will bear and rear sons, unlike her mother. There is no question of Charlotte having any choice in this matter, but the sooner she is married, the better. If she is told at fourteen she will accept the idea. She is very obedient; she will submit unquestioningly to her parents' wishes. She will make a very good wife for Georg. He and his parents are pleased at the idea of a match between Charlotte and him.'

I longed to ask more questions, to find out what Charlotte's father thought about it. That would have been impertinent on my part, though. Obviously, he must approve of the arrangement. Poor Charlotte! She was even more to be pitied than I had thought. Georg was a lecherous, hard drinking, conceited lout. Carl von Oldenburg must have a good idea of his cousin's shortcomings, in view of the fact that he was soon seeking us out after I had been made the Rain Bird. And yet, even though he knew that Georg was not to be trusted with women, he was apparently quite agreeable to allowing his young daughter to be married off to him. I felt distaste towards the whole way of life at that schloss.

'My son will probably return earlier than my daughter-in-law,' went on the Countess. 'He told me he would come back and leave her and Charlotte with his wife's family. He often does this when they visit. My daughter-in-law's parents spoil Charlotte dreadfully when they see her. It seems to be their one idea in bringing up children; we have one spoilt child in the schloss already.'

I was somewhat surprised that the Countess had made a remark like that to me, although I had no doubt it was true. Countess Maria gave the impression of being extremely spoilt; spoilt and wilful.

'Spoilt children need firm handling. I've told my son so,' went on Countess Adelaide. 'But then, it's not my place to interfere. I would not mention these things to you, Miss Burness, if I felt you were not to be trusted. Since the birth of her last son four years ago, Countess Maria has pleaded ill-health when it has suited her. She has got her own way in many matters by using this method. If my son is entertaining certain of his friends, she feigns a headache or something, simply because she is too bored to make an effort. And always she rises late; her toilet is never completed until just before *mittagessen*. My son was not brought up to such idle ways.'

He certainly was not, I reflected. 'I met him one morning when I was going to Goppertal,' I said. 'I was walking down the mountain road and it was misty. He suddenly appeared, on horseback. He told me then that he always rose early.'

'That is true. Naturally, when he was in the army he had to, and he attended a military academy before then. My son was a very fine soldier. He was one of the youngest ever to receive the Iron Cross.' I could hear the note of pride in her voice. 'He was, of course, badly wounded in the hand . . . perhaps you have noticed the scars?'

'I have,' I said, feeling a little embarrassed that she should be talking to me about her family in this way.

'The scar on his face, that is different. It was not a war wound. It was caused in a duel.'

'Oh,' I said, a little sense of shock creeping through me.

'Yes. I am afraid too many duels have been fought by the men in the von Oldenburg family. Otto fought and was killed in a duel over his gambling — I believe he had been accused of cheating at cards. And Carl was also duelling over a matter of honour.' She shook her head.

'Did he . . . er, win?' I asked, interested in spite of myself. I wanted her to go on talking about him. I knew that he was not a happy man, and I had a feeling that his mother knew it also.

'Yes, he won. He never revealed to me the cause of the duel, though. Only that he had been defending the honour of the von Oldenburgs. The scar on his face is a sabre cut.'

'They duelled with sabres?' I asked doubtfully.

'Naturally. My son was a cavalry officer; an expert swordsman.'

The honour of the von Oldenburgs, I thought. How mediaeval all this seemed. Apart from the von Oldenburgs themselves, who cared about their honour? Perhaps I was not in the best position to judge that, though. In Goppertal and the surrounding countryside they were looked up to by the peasants, and by the solid burghers, too. *Frau* Krafft had oozed pride that a pupil of hers had been engaged as a governess for Charlotte.

That night I pondered on the conversation I'd had with the Countess. However, although I spent some time with her every day, she did not discuss the family again. We talked of many things; of books and of music and of the problems of poverty, both in Germany and in England. The Countess was very concerned about the poor people in the neighbourhood. She had always supplied them with food at Christmas; both she and her son took a special interest in some of the more unfortunate families. Here again, although she did not say so in as many words, I somehow got the impression that Countess Maria took no part in such activities.

I wondered as to the nature of the Dowager Countess' illness, and if it were true that her days were numbered. Once or twice I rode into Goppertal, and enjoyed myself in the genial atmosphere of the Geisner household. Although *Frau* Geisner was such a pleasant personality, I knew that she was rather a gossip, and I was always careful never to repeat anything which I thought should not go beyond the schloss.

One evening, quite without warning, as I was sitting with Countess Adelaide,

Count von Oldenburg appeared in the room. I was quite startled and jumped up, dropping my needlework.

'I'm sorry, I didn't mean to give you a fright. I couldn't see any of the maids around and I thought the Countess might have retired,' he explained, picking up my embroidery for me.

'*Mutter* . . . ' he greeted her with a kiss, remarking that I seemed more startled than she at seeing him arrive home unexpectedly. He said he would go back to Karismette in a few days and return with his wife and Charlotte.

'No doubt they are enjoying themselves,' remarked the Countess, a faint note of disapproval in her voice. No, it was not disapproval, I decided. It was more a kind of sad resignation, as though for her the days of active enjoyment were over. She became more cheerful when her son asked how she had been during his absence.

'Better than of late, I think. *Fraulein* Burness has been a splendid companion and has shown me all the work which has been done in your father's garden. It should be ready to sit in again by next summer.'

'Yes, next summer you will sit in it,' said her son, smiling. But as he spoke I saw the anguish in his eyes. I realised then how deeply he loved her, and that her days were indeed numbered. I had a feeling that he had come back earlier than expected because he had not wanted to leave her alone in the schloss for too long, even though I was keeping her company. He began to talk about their visit to his wife's family, obviously telling his mother small items of news and gossip which he thought might interest her. Feeling slightly embarrassed, I suggested that he and the Countess might prefer to talk together, and picked up my embroidery, ready to leave the room.

'Unless you particularly wish to leave our company,' said the Count, 'there is no reason why you should . . . is there?' He appealed to his mother.

'Indeed, you must stay with us,

Fraulein Burness, and join in the conversation,' said Countess Adelaide warmly. Between them they put me at my ease and I asked how Charlotte was getting on and what she had been doing.

'She is being spoilt,' he assured me. 'Her mother relaxes discipline when she is with her own family. She can scarcely do anything else; there is a great outcry from them if Charlotte is denied anything.'

'Yes, I can imagine so,' said his mother, shaking her head. 'At least Maria makes a firm stand with Charlotte when she is at home.'

'I don't think that a bit of spoiling will do Charlotte any harm,' I said, thinking even as I spoke that I was being impertinent.

'Indeed?' The Count looked at me and I could feel myself flushing under his keen gaze.

'I mean . . . I do not think that she has the sort of nature which could easily be spoilt,' I said hastily.

'I think perhaps *Fraulein* Burness could be right,' conceded his mother. 'After all, she will be fourteen next birthday. Probably by now her character has already been moulded.'

I felt like adding that it didn't matter anyway, if she was destined to marry her rakish, philandering cousin, Georg von Oldenburg. And why bother about her education, deportment and everything else they bothered about? The Count himself was a man of some culture, despite his military background. But his cousin Georg cared for nothing except hunting, drinking, womanising and gambling, from what I had seen and heard. So why should his future wife have to conform to such rigid standards? I thought again of the night I had seen Countess Maria walking in the grounds with another man. *She* did not set much of an example to her daughter, anyway.

The Count was talking again of this and that. Of picnics and other excursions and of balls which they had attended. Before the evening was over I mentioned that, as Charlotte was still away, I would like to go back to the *Damenstift* to spend a few days there. *Frau* Krafft had told me that I was welcome there any time.

'If that is what you want, certainly you may,' said the Count. 'You have been most kind, keeping my mother company in our absence. In fact, I wonder how we managed before you came.'

I was surprised when he said this, but I could tell from the expression on his face that he was quite sincere. Somehow I found sleep difficult that night. Very early the following morning, straight after breakfast, I went out for a walk. The earth was wet with dew. I left the grounds of the schloss and walked a little way down the mountain road. Foxgloves were blooming in profusion everywhere. It was Sunday, and suddenly I heard the first church bells of the day peal forth and echo round the mountains. For a few moments I stood still, listening. There was a footstep behind me.

'Good day, *Fraulein* Burness. I saw you walking ahead and caught you up,' said the Count.

'Good day, Your Excellency.' He stood beside me and I was suddenly aware of my heart beating too quickly. I knew that he would start to speak in his laboured, halting English and, sure enough, he did.

'I know that you make your own . . . plans on a Sunday, but if you are thinking of going to church you would perhaps consider accomp — accomp — coming with us today? My mother said she would go today. She has not attend — attended church for some weeks.'

He stood looking down at me while the bells echoed all around. I lowered my gaze. Was it my imagination, or was his scarred hand trembling slightly? Something inside me was trembling; that I knew beyond all doubt.

'Thank you,' I heard myself say. 'I

will accompany you in the coach if you would like it.'

'I wish it,' he said simply in English. 'My mother also.'

I struggled to regain my composure. 'Yes, very well,' I said briskly. 'When shall I be ready?'

'In half an hour. Those are not our church bells ringing.'

'I'll go back and get ready now.' I was wearing a skirt and blouse, a somewhat old blouse at that. I turned and retraced my footsteps into the grounds of the schloss, leaving him staring after me. At least, I thought he was, although I didn't look round. He was clearly already dressed to attend church; immaculate from his shining blonde head down to his gleaming boots. At the last minute, Heinrich would hand him his hat, kid gloves and prayer book . . .

Why was I hurrying so? Why was I trembling? Back in my *boudoir* the mirror reflected my flushed face and shining eyes. There was a great unrest within me, and a great fear, too. Some time later, attired in a plain grey gown and bonnet, I was seated in one of the von Oldenburg carriages. I recognised it as being the dark green one in which Siegfried had first driven me to the schloss. He was driving now. The vehicle teetered at a precarious angle going down the steep, rough road, but the horses were well used to it. The Countess and her son sat opposite me. The Count's blue eyes kept catching mine in a gaze which set my heart pounding. The Countess kept up a flow of conversation, to which I replied when necessary. She was explaining that the von Oldenburgs at one time attended their private chapel in the castle, but now it was no longer in use as such, and they preferred to go into the town to worship. I myself had never attended morning service at the church, but I had been several times on a Sunday evening with the Geisner family. The Count asked me if I had ever seen the private chapel at the schloss, and I said that Charlotte had shown me it one day. I added that I had been very impressed by the exquisite wood carving in it.

'It still has an atmosphere of great peace,' said the Count, his eyes on me again in that disconcerting way. Peace was the last thing I experienced on that journey. My thoughts were in turmoil and it was a relief when we arrived at the beautiful old church with its Gothic walls, baroque dome and magnificent stained glass windows. The von Oldenburgs had their own pew and the three of us took our places in it. I sat between the Count and his mother and I felt as though a spell had been cast on me.

Back at the schloss, the Count suggested that I should join him and his mother at *nachtessen* that evening.

'Thank you — it is kind of you, but I do not mind having my meals alone in the schoolroom,' I said nervously.

'Perhaps not, but I think you should have *nachtessen* with us while Charlotte is away.' His mouth closed firmly and I thought it better to fall in with his wishes. For the rest of the day I kept away from the von Oldenburgs.

Changing into old clothes, I put on thick gloves and continued with the weeding of the late Count's garden. As I did so, I could think of nothing but his son and the way he had looked at me that morning: and more that that, how I had felt. I straightened up and took a deep breath. It was as though I had finally accepted something which I had pretended was not happening. I was in love with Carl von Oldenburg, a German Count and a married man. Something which I had never dreamed possible had happened. I thought of my uncle's wise words, warning me to be careful when I took this position at Schloss Beissel. How does one be careful not to fall in love?

I must return to England; there was no other way. I could not stay at Schloss Beissel. I would have to make up some excuse for leaving. I could not return to England, though. I could not bear to leave him. I gave up weeding and went indoors. My restless feet took me to the schoolroom. How empty it seemed without Charlotte's bright head bending over her books; Charlotte, his daughter . . .

I discarded my thick gloves and sat down, staring ahead of me. I loved him; I loved him. The words seemed to burn into my very soul. And he, did he love me in return? Why had he looked at me like that if he didn't? But Georg had looked at me like that; what did such glances signify coming from the von Oldenburg men? Perhaps, after all, Carl von Oldenburg was no better than his cousin. And what of his wife, Countess Maria? She flirted behind her husband's back; or did he know? Thoughts like these whirled through my head as I sat there, but one thought was more powerful than any of the others. I loved him.

That evening I joined the Count and his mother for *nachtessen*. In Germany, even in the highest circles, *mittagessen* was the main meal of the day, and the von Oldenburgs were no exception. They dressed formally for *mittagessen* and again in the evening for *nachtessen*, a meal which began rather curiously with tea and cakes and cold viands making the first course, followed by varieties of hot entrees and sweets.

Trembling inwardly, I sat at the flower-bedecked, beautifully-laid table in that great dining room with its limewood ceiling, a riot of grotesques and acanthus. Although the schloss dated from mediaeval times, much had been added to it with the passing generations of von Oldenburgs. Oil portraits of these long-dead ancestors seemed to watch me silently from the dark, panelled walls.

Countess Adelaide was dressed in a grey gown, a cap of finest lace on her head. Her hands were white with raised, purple veins and the great diamond rings on her long, thin fingers sparkled like living fire in the candlelight.

I was wearing a simple gown of blue organza, which she was kind enough to say suited me.

'It does indeed,' agreed her son, his eyes catching mine again in that disconcerting, intimate way. I held the cool stem of my wineglass in a hand which was not steady, occasionally joining in the conversation. Carl von Oldenburg's voice washed over me in waves.

'Tell me which day you are planning to go back to your old school. I will escort you to Goppertal station myself.'

'Please — do not trouble,' I murmured, knowing that I was colouring up.

'It is no trouble,' said the Count quietly.

'It will be a pleasant change for you, *Fraulein* Burness,' put in his mother. 'I am sure you must have found the schloss very quiet without Charlotte. It is well that you have friends you are able to visit in Goppertal.'

'Indeed? I did not know that you had

friends in the town,' said the Count, raising his eyebrows.

'I am friendly with Charlotte's music teacher, *Frau* Geisner, and with her daughter, Emma,' I explained.

'The Geisners are good people, well respected in Goppertal,' remarked Carl von Oldenburg, looking distinctly relieved. 'I know it is rather a difficult position for a young English lady to find herself shut away in a schloss with no companionship of her own age. It would be quite easy for her to cultivate undesirable friends without realising it.'

'*Fraulein* Burness is far too sensible for that,' was his mother's comment.

So that was what she thought me; sensible. Little did she know the secret of my heart. Little did she know that I was sitting there trembling because her son was sitting at the same table. After we had dined we withdrew to a richly-furnished sitting room with crimson damask silks on the walls and furniture. There was also a beautiful piano and, rather to my surprise, the

Count sat down and began to play for us. He seemed to be a competent pianist to me, but his mother told me in a low voice that he could not play as he once had, before his hand had been wounded. She added though that his determination to play the piano again had been a great help in his recovery. As she was telling me this he caught my eye and smiled.

'Charlotte is very musical,' I said afterwards. 'She has a very pretty singing voice, too.'

'Yes, I have noticed that. I have always been most insistent that she should have a good musical education.'

'She could not be in better hands than with *Frau* Geisner,' I said.

'Talking of hands,' said the Count, 'I see Charlotte seems to have given up that appalling habit of biting her nails since you have been with us.'

'Yes. I only hope she has not started it again while she has been away.'

'She does not appear to have.'

'No, because she is growing up now,'

said the Countess. 'She is turning into a young lady.'

I saw a look of sadness on the Count's face. 'She will be a young lady soon enough,' he said.

I felt that it was time for me to retire. The Countess was looking rather drawn. I thought that sometimes she suffered pain, but I knew that she was not the type of woman to show it.

That night I lay wakeful in bed for a long time. As I turned over restlessly I wondered what on earth I should do. I could tell the Count was aware of me in the same way that I was aware of him. Suppose he made an advance; what would I do then? I would have to repulse him, make that an excuse for leaving. Yes . . . I could do that.

Even as I thought about it, I longed with a passionate longing to feel his arms around me and his lips pressed hard on mine. I wanted to run my fingers through his golden hair, to caress him, to kiss that sabre scar on his face. All my theories about how I was going to conduct my life had ended in confusion. I had not reckoned with a passion like this sweeping into it and changing everything. I was obsessed with the man. I could think of little else. The pain and joy of being in close proximity to him was almost unbearable.

I had taken a long time to perform my toilet that evening because I had wanted to look my best. Yes, I had wanted him to look at me and admire me. I was frightened and ashamed, miserable and madly happy, all at once.

5

A few days later I sat in the carriage with the Count as he accompanied me to Goppertal. I was looking forward to seeing *Frau* Krafft again, but at the same time I was loath to leave the schloss. The day started by being misty and then turned crystal clear. It was late summer, with just a hint of autumn in the air.

I had recently received a letter from Alistair, giving me news of Southsands and telling me about the holiday he had recently taken in Scotland. At first he had addressed me as 'Dear Miss Burness', then 'Dear Marnie' in his letters. But now the letters began, 'Dearest Marnie', and endearments had started to creep into them. When my aunt wrote she would unfailingly mention him and what a help he was to my uncle.

As I sat in the carriage with Carl von Oldenburg, I found myself trying to compare him with Alistair Harlow, and giving it up as impossible.

'You are very quiet, Miss Burness,' said the Count slowly, speaking in English.

'I am thinking,' I replied.

'That is a great occupation,' he said, lapsing into German. 'I suppose I may not ask what you are thinking about?'

I smiled. 'I am thinking about England,' I admitted. 'I have just received a letter from — ' I paused — 'from the young doctor who assists my uncle.'

'You have not received unpleasant news, I hope?'

'No. Well, he mentioned that my aunt seems to have been a bit tired lately, but I don't think there is any cause to worry, or my uncle would have let me know.'

'Older ladies often feel tired, but that is not an illness. So you write to this young doctor?'

'Yes. We started writing some time ago, when I was still a pupil at the *Damenstift*. He is very dedicated to his work.'

'Dedication is a wonderful thing. I too was dedicated once.'

'You mean . . . to being a soldier?' I asked dubiously.

'Yes. You think that strange?'

I felt rather as if I had been trapped. 'No, I suppose not,' I said hurriedly.

'But you think it is more worthwhile to save life than to be prepared to take it?' He was extremely perceptive; that was exactly what I had been thinking.

'It does seem so,' I admitted.

'But you have an army in your own country — and a navy. If men are not prepared to die for their own country — if men are not prepared to fight in times of war — what would happen to the women — to the old people — to the children?'

'I don't know,' I said in some confusion. 'I mean, well, I know that what you say is true. I just wish there were no wars.'

'The von Oldenburgs have always had a good military record,' he said simply. 'It is expected of a second son that he should enter a military academy.'

'I enjoyed the military balls I sometimes attended in Leiknar when I was at school,' I said. 'The young officers were very merry company, and most charming.'

'I was stationed at Leiknar for some time when I was very young. I know the place well.'

His blue eyes were burning into mine. The close proximity of his presence in the carriage was a heady sensation. If he had leaned forward and clasped my hands, what would I have done? The very thought of it made my senses reel. He did not lean forward and clasp my hands, though. Instead he went back to the beginning of our conversation.

'You are friendly with this young doctor who assists your uncle, then?'

'Yes. My aunt and uncle are very fond of him.'

'I see.' He paused a moment before speaking again. 'And you, *Fraulein* Burness, you are fond of him too, I suppose?'

I could feel myself flushing at such a personal question. How dare he ask me such a thing? The atmosphere in the carriage seemed to be charged with emotion.

I replied non-committally that he was very nice.

The Count gave a brief smile, but I saw the pain and unhappiness in his eyes. Did he mind if I was fond of another man? He had no right to ask me such a personal question. Suppose I asked him if he was fond of his wife, and she of him? But no, I was merely his daughter's governess. I could not ask such impertinent questions.

'Perhaps you already have an understanding with him?'

'You are very interested, Your Excellency,' I said reprovingly.

'You must forgive me. You have such different ideas about everything. You are so independent. I have never met a young lady like you before. At first my wife complained about your English ways and the fact that you brought some changes to the schoolroom. But Charlotte has done so well since you have been with us that she says little now. The schloss must have seemed a strange place to you at first. You are like a fresh English breeze blowing through it, and yet you were willing to take part in our local festival; you did not object to being the Rain Bird for the evening.'

I was uncomfortably reminded of the way he had rescued me from his cousin Georg.

'No, I did not mind,' I said. 'Such things are enjoyable. That is, as long as people do not drink too much and behave foolishly.'

He frowned. 'I know what you mean. There was little chance of that, though, at the schloss. My cousin Georg is fond of practical jokes, I know. That is why I followed him, as I did not want you to be alarmed at all.'

'I was grateful to you,' I said. Why was he mentioning the incident now? Did he think, or did he perhaps hope, that Georg had not been in earnest? I knew differently, but I was not going to say so.

We were in Goppertal now and driving along the quaint, cobbled streets to the station. The coachman drew the horses to a halt and alighted to open the carriage door. The Count helped me down from the vehicle and the touch of his hand filled me with unbearable joy. The coachman carried my valise to the train and put it on the rack. The Count removed his hat and stood bare-headed to wave me off.

I sat back in the seat and tried to collect my thoughts as the train steamed out. I was hopelessly in love with a married man. I must leave Charlotte, leave the schloss and go back to England. My aunt and uncle would be pleased to see me; Alistair Harlow would be more than pleased. To remain at Schloss Beissel could bring only suffering to myself and others . . .

Did the Count care for me? And if he did, what difference would it make anyway? He was married. Did he perhaps think he could treat me the way his cousin Georg would have liked? I caught my breath at the thought of being clasped in the Count's arms. What would my aunt and uncle think if they knew? When I had made the decision to come to the schloss as Charlotte's governess I had not dreamed of anything like this. These emotions, these powerful, terrible emotions sweeping through me . . .

Charlotte's father — yes, the father of a thirteen-year-old girl, and a foreigner withal; a German aristocrat with German ideas and ways. How could I be in love with him? Perhaps it was not love; perhaps it was what people called infatuation. But if it was, how did you tell the difference? You only knew that you felt these emotions.

In a way it was a relief to get away from the schloss, although already I was missing the physical presence of the Count. I was alone in the carriage, for which I was grateful. Perhaps under the benign influence of *Frau* Krafft I might see things differently.

She was there on the platform to meet me, as endearingly untidy as ever. We embraced in the late summer sunshine and soon I was being driven off in the wagonette, listening to all the gossip about the school.

Then she questioned me eagerly about my life at the schloss. I told her of the strict way Charlotte was being brought up and how I thought she would be expected to marry very young, and not to a man of her choice.

'I sometimes feel that teaching her good English is rather a waste,' I said.

'Never. Nothing is wasted. But apart from that, you are settled there?'

I hesitated. How could I be settled there under the circumstances?

'I can't really say that. There are so many things I don't approve of. It's a beautiful place, of course.'

'But you are well treated by the von Oldenburgs?'

'Yes. And I've made friends with a family in Goppertal.'

'So you are happy?'

'Well, in a way . . . '

'In a way? You don't seem truly happy, Marnie.' She sounded reproachful.

I longed to cry out: 'How can I be truly happy when I am in love with a married man? How can I stay there?' I could not do that, though. 'There are so many things I don't like about the place,' I said. 'The Countess is a strange woman. The Count's brother was to have married her, but he was killed in a duel just before their wedding, so the present Count married her instead. It all seems so odd, somehow.'

'Not really, I suppose. Evidently they had decided that she was to be the next Countess.'

'How cold-blooded! What place does love have in the scheme of things?'

'It has no place with these aristocratic families. Titles, money, land; these are

117

the important things with such families.'

'But the Countess seems so unsuitable,' I said. 'She takes little interest in anything apart from her own enjoyment, and she's terribly indolent. She speaks only German herself, but she insists on her daughter being fluent in three languages. I've changed a few ideas in the schoolroom because I didn't agree with them.'

'And the daughter — is she like her mother?'

'No, altogether different. She's much more intellectual and much more industrious. She's inclined to be nervous and highly-strung, but she's a sweet child.'

'Perhaps she takes after the Count.'

'I think she does. He has features like his mother and the girl has similar features. I think she is going to grow into a woman rather like her grandmother in many ways, not just physically.'

'Her grandmother is a different type of woman from the young Countess Maria, then?'

'Altogether different. And she does

not appear to like her daughter-in-law very much. I can't imagine her wanting her son to marry Countess Maria at all.'

'Very strange indeed,' commented *Frau* Krafft. 'But now, let us talk of other things. Tell me how things are with your people in England.'

I sat in her room with her, drinking coffee and listening to her well-remembered voice.

'My aunt and uncle are quite well,' I said. 'My aunt has been a bit tired lately, that's all.'

'And the young doctor who assists your uncle? You used to receive letters from him when you were here.'

'Yes. He still writes.'

'It is good to receive letters from home. It would not surprise me if you returned to England one day and married that young man, despite your independent ideas.'

'Oh, *Frau* Krafft, you are as bad as my aunt! I think she would like me to do that.'

'And what better could you do, my dear? For people who heal the sick, no praise is too high. To be the wife of such a man, and to give him the support he needs in his daily life, is not a calling to be sneered at. I am not disparaging the profession of teaching, far from it, but you could end up by being very lonely, Marnie. I would understand if you chose love. *Ach*, yes, I too have loved.'

'Yes, I know you have. But . . . ' I broke off. How could I tell this kindly German woman that I was in love with one of her countrymen, one who was my employer, and a married man to boot? I was in an impossible situation and there was no-one with whom I could share the secret of my heart. I changed the subject.

The next few days went quickly. *Frau* Krafft had arranged for me to sleep in the same little room I had slept in when I had been a pupil there. I was touched by her kindness. As always, she took the new girls on a picnic, to the same place we went when Isabel and I had been new pupils there. I went with them and it was very nostalgic. The school had not changed, nor had *Frau* Krafft. I had changed, though.

When the time came for me to return to the schloss I parted from *Frau* Krafft with mixed feelings. I had enjoyed my stay there, but all the time I had been wondering how things were at Schloss Beissel and whether the Count had missed me. For I had missed him with an intensity which appalled me. He had been insistent that I should write and say when I would be returning, so that he could have a carriage sent to meet me. However, I was totally unprepared to see him waiting on the platform when the train steamed into Goppertal Station. Nor was he alone; his daughter stood beside him.

'*Fraulein* Burness! How are you? How pleasant to see you again,' he exclaimed in English. 'I have been back to Karismette, as you can see, and brought Charlotte home. Her mother is prolonging her stay for another week or two.'

'It is very kind of you to meet me, Your Excellency, and to bring Charlotte,' I replied in some confusion. The pleasure on his face was matched by that of his daughter. The emotions which rose in me were so strong that for a moment I could not speak; it was like being welcomed back home. The coachman took my valise and we walked out of the station to the waiting carriage.

'Is your mother, the Countess, fairly well?' I enquired of the Count.

'She does not complain. She takes a short walk in the grounds when she is well enough. She has been to inspect your garden.' He smiled.

'I think she is pleased about it,' I said.

'Yes. I keep telling her that she will sit in it again next summer.' His face became sad when he said this and I knew that his mother's illness was a heavy burden for him to carry.

Charlotte looked very well and I began to ask her questions about her stay in Karismette, speaking in English.

I complimented her on the fact that her nails were still unbitten. As we drove up the mountain road I realised that the three of us were happy together. The Count seemed pleased at the way his daughter answered my questions in English.

At last the carriage bowled through the familiar portals of the castle and into the cobbled courtyard. The mighty round tower loomed up, huge and menacing, reminding me again that Schloss Beissel had been built originally as a fortress. I entered the great door of the castle with mixed emotions.

'I've missed you,' said Charlotte shyly, as soon as her father left us. I told her, quite truthfully, that I had missed her, too. A pang shot through me at the thought that I might have to leave her, yet how much less would that pain be than the anguish of leaving her father!

The following day we settled down to lessons again, but now every morning the Count appeared in the schoolroom, ostensibly to see how his daughter was progressing at her studies. That was not the most important reason, though. His blue eyes would meet mine and I would feel the magnetism of his physical presence to such an extent that my heart would beat violently.

Charlotte and I still worked in the garden, but now her father often came to join us. The three of us would talk and work together and Charlotte seemed to be losing some of her awe for her father; in fact, they were drawing closer. The Count was relaxed and happy in the garden with us; for me the joy of having him close to me mingled with the fear of my own feelings.

The Dowager Countess had asked me if I would sometimes visit her rooms to talk to her and I made a point of doing this occasionally. She seemed to enjoy my companionship, despite the difference in our ages.

The fine weather continued. One afternoon the Count appeared in the schoolroom and announced that the following day he was going to drive

Charlotte and me to his hunting lodge in the forest.

'A day without lessons — for both of you,' he said, smiling.

'Thank you very much, Your Excellency. I shall look forward to it,' I said, my heart beginning to pound with pleasurable excitement. His daughter was delighted, too. She had never been there before, which surprised me a little. Then I realised that it would be a most unlikely place to take Charlotte; after all, what man would take his young daughter so such a masculine stronghold as a hunting lodge? Then why was he taking her now . . . and me? The answer was not hard to find. He wanted to take us somewhere away from the schloss to a place where we could be close together. I knew in my heart that he wanted to be alone with me, but he was bound to include his daughter for the sake of appearances.

We left the schloss the following morning in a trap driven by one of the young grooms. I wore my dove-grey travelling costume, and both Charlotte and I took cloaks in case it turned cold later in the day. The Count was dressed in sturdy tweeds and looked as excited as we were. We drove downhill from the plateau on which the castle was built, and it was soon hidden from our view by the trees. Never had the scenery appeared as magnificent as it did on that golden morning; the silver and spruce firs, the rush of a waterfall, even the familiar tinkle of cowbells had never sounded so sweet.

The Count gave me a swiftly-appraising glance, which told me that I was looking my best. Just for a few precious hours I wanted to forget that he was married. I only wanted to feel the intense emotion of being close to him, of seeing him smile at me, of knowing that he was happy too. So was Charlotte. Her eyes were bright with pleasure as she sat in the trap, enjoying her outing.

The Count pointed out places of interest and talked about the hunting which he expected to be doing soon. We branched off before we reached Goppertal and took a rather rough road which was unfamiliar to me. Down the mountain slope we went. Every now and then we would reach a plateau, with a farmhouse inevitably situated there. Everything was exciting; the forest smells, the distant lowing of cattle, a silvery stream glimpsed through trees.

'Won't Mama be surprised when she knows where I have been?' asked Charlotte artlessly. 'Why have you never taken Mama and me to the hunting lodge?'

'I doubt if your Mama would be very interested,' replied her father. 'Anyway, she has probably been in a hunting lodge at some time in her life. But you must remember that *Fraulein* Burness is English, and that it is of interest to her to visit a German hunting lodge.'

Because of the state of my emotions, there was something comical about his telling Charlotte that I would be interested in visiting a hunting lodge. I could not repress a little laugh. I caught the Count's eye and, rather to my surprise, he laughed too. 'Look,' he said, indicating a tiny village below us. 'That is Fendorf, one of the last places where they burnt a witch.'

'They don't burn witches now, do they?' asked Charlotte anxiously.

We both assured her that they didn't.

'You are not thinking of being a witch, I hope?' asked the Count, looking worried.

'Oh, no, Papa.' Charlotte seemed quite shocked.

'Your father is teasing you,' I said gently. 'My uncle was always teasing me when I was your age.'

She looked relieved and shot a shy glance at her father. Clearly she was quite unused to anything like that from him. We were entering more deeply into the forest and the Count said it would not be long before we arrived at the hunting lodge. When we first saw it, situated in a clearing, it looked smaller than I had expected. It was of grey stone with latticed windows; a solid-looking place with stables at the side of it. Charlotte cried out with pleasure, saying that it was a dear little house. The groom halted the horses, alighted and opened the door of the trap. The Count stepped out and, reaching up, lifted his daughter down, giving her a little swing round as he did so. Then he extended his hand to me.

Stone steps led up to the heavy, iron-studded door of the lodge, above which was the von Oldenburg emblem. Just as we were about to enter, it was opened from within by a fat, middle-aged woman.

'Welcome, Master,' she said, curtsey-ing. We were welcomed into a hall containing a large, solid table. There was a big fireplace with unlit pine logs in the grate and the floor was of polished boards with rugs made out of animals' skins scattered about. A man who appeared to be in his sixties came into the room and greeted the Count, bowing as he did so. The Count explained that they were Inga and Josef, who lived at the lodge and cooked and waited on the huntsmen during the season. It was obvious that they had known about our visit beforehand. A meal was prepared for the three of us and Inga waited at table. The groom had disappeared with her husband; no doubt he would be having *mittagessen* in the servants' quarters.

It was plain, but excellent food. We had *sauerbraten*, followed by *dampf-nudeln*, a delicious, but rather filling pudding. The Count and I had Mosel wine with our food. The fat, jolly Inga produced a home-made cordial for Charlotte, who was quite entranced with the hunting lodge, the meal and everything else.

The Count told me that the hunting lodge was quite old, and that it had always belonged to the von Oldenburg family. He added that Inga and Josef had known him all his life. It was plain from the way that Inga fussed over him that she was fond of him, and Charlotte enjoyed being thoroughly spoilt and listening to Inga's many stories of the forest.

'Come, we'll go for a walk,' said the Count and the three of us set off, with Charlotte walking between us. The sunlight filtered through the trees; birds swooped and soared and sang overhead. A busy squirrel scampered from behind a tree and we were conscious of bright, unseen eyes watching us from a myriad hiding places. The utter stillness of the forest, apart from the faint breeze which sighed in the tree tops, made us feel more securely cut off from the rest of the world than when we were in the hunting lodge. Somehow I did not feel like talking much. I was happy, with a wonderful all-pervading happiness, which looked neither to the past nor the future. Charlotte prattled on about Inga's stories, some of which I knew as German folklore.

'Where are you taking us, Papa?' she enquired.

'I want to show you both something,'

was the reply. Certainly he seemed to know this part of the forest, otherwise I would not have been keen on venturing into such a thickly-wooded area. It would be far too easy to get lost. The next moment Charlotte gave a little squeal of delight. 'Look! There's a little house! Look, *Fraulein* Burness!'

She hurried forward. Her father watched her, smiling indulgently. I suddenly stumbled over a tree root and felt his hand grasping my arm immediately.

'Be careful. The ground is a bit rough in parts,' he said.

'Thank you. I nearly fell.' The hard clasp of his hand on my arm had set my heart thudding wildly. He did not release me altogether, but slipped his arm through mine for the remaining few yards to the little house ahead. It was made of logs.

'Windows with no glass in them — and a ladder to go upstairs,' said Charlotte in amazement. 'Who lives here?'

'Nobody now. Nobody ever since I first saw this place when I was a boy,' said her father. 'But you know the story Inga told you, of a princess who ran off with a woodcutter and came to live in the forest with him . . . '

'And she lived here?' Charlotte's eye were wide with wonder.

'So Inga says.'

The three of us explored it. It had clearly been built a long time ago; it must have been someone's house at one time, but it was completely derelict now. Charlotte wanted to climb up the old ladder to see in the room upstairs, but we would not allow her to. Nevertheless, she scampered about, getting her hands and dress quite soiled in the process.

'The forest is full of surprises,' said the Count.

'It is indeed. I would not be too astonished to come across a gingerbread house,' I said, laughing.

'I think we had better be making our way back now. Come, Charlotte.'

We retraced our footsteps. I noticed that a mist was rising. As we walked along it grew thicker. I began to feel uneasy.

'Don't worry, I know the landmarks,' said the Count cheerfully. 'I shall be very careful not to take the wrong turning.'

'We won't get lost, will we, Papa?' Charlotte looked anxious.

'Of course not. Let's link arms so that we can't lose each other.'

We walked along like this with Charlotte in the middle. 'It's an exciting adventure,' I told her. At the same time I sincerely hoped that her father could find his way back to the hunting lodge, as the mist was getting more and more dense. It was eerie now, walking along through the silent, sunless forest. I pictured the three of us becoming hopelessly lost. Still, lost people were supposed to walk in a circle. Did that mean we would eventually reach the hunting lodge if we kept on walking, or would we find ourselves back at the funny little house?

The next moment Charlotte and I both cried out, as a light suddenly shone out of the mist in front of us. It was Josef; he had known where the Count would most likely take us and had come with a lantern to look for us.

'Everything's all right now,' said the Count reassuringly. 'Even if you didn't trust me to find the way back, you should feel safe now Josef is here.'

We were soon back at the hunting lodge, but the mist settled down so densely that it was plain we could not return to the schloss as planned.

'We shall have to spend the night here,' said the Count. 'Inga and Josef will look after us.'

Charlotte was excited at the prospect. So was I. I asked him if our absence would cause any concern at the schloss, but he assured me that it would not. His valet knew where we had gone; it would be assumed that we had stayed overnight at the hunting lodge because of the misty conditions.

The pine logs were now crackling and glowing in the hearth, as the night promised to be chilly. Inga prepared a simple meal for us; cold chicken, fruit and cheeses with crusty bread and excellent coffee.

'I will show you to your room, *fraulein*,' she said. Charlotte and I followed her up the bare, wooden stairs, our shadows enormous in the flickering light of her candle.

'I have prepared it for when you are ready. See.' We entered a room containing a large bed, a dressing-table and many cupboards. A welcoming fire was burning in the grate. Inga lit two more candles in their sconces over the dressing-table. 'I have put out two nightgowns' she went on. 'One belongs to one of my grandchildren; the other one is mine. It is for you to wear, *fraulein*.'

I thanked her, saying that we would be very comfortable. There was a ewer and wash basin and other toilet equipment.

'I don't have to go to bed yet, do I?' enquired Charlotte. I assured her that she could stay up for a while longer, and Inga chuckled.

'I like it here,' announced Charlotte as we left the bedroom. 'Where will Papa sleep?'

Inga indicated a room opposite ours on the landing. 'That is your Papa's room. It always has been.'

To my surprise when we went downstairs again, Josef was sitting in a corner of the room with a fiddle in his hand. There were three chairs drawn up in front of the roaring fire and the Count told us that Josef was going to play for us. Inga curtseyed and bade us goodnight, leaving her husband to entertain us. He began to play and I soon realised that he played surprisingly well. I had no doubt that he was much in demand when the lodge was full of huntsmen.

The Count poured out wine for himself and me; Josef was drinking beer and Charlotte, cordial. We sat in the firelight while the sharp, sweet notes of the fiddle rose and fell from the corner. The Count told Charlotte she could ask for all her favourite tunes, which she did, and Josef played them one after another. Then I caught her trying to stifle a yawn, which was not surprising after a day spent in the fresh air.

'Come, Charlotte, it is time for bed,' I said.

'But you will not retire yet?' The Count's eyes met mine.

'No . . . no, I'll come down for a little while longer.'

Charlotte kissed her father, thanked Josef courteously for his playing and bade both the men goodnight. I took her up to the bedroom. The nightgown which Inga had provided was rather skimpy on her, but it served well enough. As she was putting it on I picked up the other nightgown from the bed and examined it curiously. Inga had said that it was hers, but it was of finest lawn and exquisitely embroidered. Moreover, it would certainly not have fitted her; it was for a slender woman. Feeling puzzled and vaguely uneasy I put it down and kissed Charlotte goodnight, telling her that I would not be late to bed. I glanced at myself in the dressing-table mirror. My hair had been damped by the mist and my face was framed with curly little tendrils. I picked up the comb thoughtfully provided by Inga.

'Don't make your hair all tidy again,' came Charlotte's voice from the depth of the enormous bed. 'It looks so pretty like that.'

'Very well,' I said with a little laugh.

'Why don't you let it down?' asked Charlotte.

For a moment I hesitated. Then, with a few swift movements I released my hair and it fell in soft waves down to my waist.

'You look beautiful, *Fraulein* Burness,' came a rather sleepy voice from the bed.

I descended the stairs again, my heart thumping painfully. When I entered the room again the Count rose to his feet, looking rather as if he had seen an apparition.

'*Fraulein* Burness! Why, you — ' he broke off. The sight of me with my hair down had clearly affected him; whatever he had been going to say, he hastily checked himself.

'My hair got very damp in the mist; I was going to put it to rights, but Charlotte suggested I should let it down. It is probably a good idea; it will be thoroughly dry by the time I go to bed.'

'A wise thought. You must not go to bed with damp hair,' said the Count, recovering his composure. 'Josef will play a little longer,' he said.

I sat down and Josef took up his fiddle again. He no longer played the merry tunes which Charlotte had asked for, though. Instead, sweet throbbing notes filled the warm, pine-fragrant air with the tremulous beauty and sadness of German *Lieder*. The sight of the Count sitting there in the firelight, the effect of the wine and my aching need for this man was suddenly too much for me. I sat without speaking, aware that the tears were slowly gathering in my eyes. The music seemed to have a special message for me; telling me without words of the beauty and pain I was experiencing in my life, and bringing home to me all the sorrow of loving one who could never be mine.

'Why, *Fraulein* Burness, you are upset,' exclaimed the Count. I could hear the note of concern in his voice.

'I'm sorry,' I managed to say, forcing a somewhat watery smile. 'Perhaps it's the sad music, or perhaps it's because I'm tired.' A tear rolled down my cheek and I fumbled in vain for a handkerchief. I must have left it on the dressing-table.

'Here,' said the Count gently. He offered me a handkerchief of fine white cambric. 'It has been a tiring day for you. I would not wish to detain you under the circumstances. I expect you would prefer to retire. Josef will play a little longer for me.'

'Thanks,' I murmured, dabbing my eyes. 'And thank you, Josef for playing so beautifully.' I withdrew from the room. The sound of the Count's '*Gute Nacht*' seemed to follow me upstairs.

I entered the bedroom quietly. The fire was dying down and Charlotte was sound asleep. I prepared for bed and put on the exquisite nightgown which Inga had left for me. It smelled of lavender. I extinguished the candle and climbed into the bed beside Charlotte. Sleep was long in coming, though. It had been a memorable day in my life. I could not have put into words the emotions which I had felt since the three of us had set off from the schloss that morning.

The way the Count had looked at me; the touch of his hand; of his arm slipped through mine; the look in his eyes when I had returned from seeing Charlotte to bed, with my hair down, and falling in waves to my waist. I turned over cautiously so as not to disturb the sleeping child. Why had Josef played that sad, tender music? Why had I wept so unexpectedly? What would have happened if I had stayed downstairs longer? Would Josef have withdrawn discreetly and left us alone together? I caught my breath at the thought. Far better that things had worked out the way they had.

After a long time I heard footsteps on the stairs. I strained my ears, listening. The footsteps seemed to pause outside our bedroom door. I lay, scarcely daring to breathe. I knew beyond all doubt that the Count was standing on the other side of that stout, heavy door. The yearning to slip out of bed and open the door silently was almost unbearable. Or would he open the door and stand there, waiting for me? But I remained in bed and the door was not opened by him. I heard another door being closed and knew that he had retired for the night. Eventually I fell asleep in that delicate, lavender-scented nightgown, which Inga had said was hers.

The following morning I examined it afresh in the daylight. The exquisite needlework, the tiny tucks and lace insertions intrigued me so much that I felt I must mention the garment to Inga. The plain fact of the matter was that I didn't believe it belonged to her. And if not to her, to whom did it belong? My opportunity to find out came early, when she tapped on the bedroom door with hot water for Charlotte and me. She asked how we had slept.

'Very well, thank you,' I replied, which was not strictly true of myself at all events. 'What a charming night-gown, Inga. It is really beautiful.'

'Always I have kept it,' she said smiling. 'Before I married I was in service with a family in Goppertal. My mistress gave me that for a wedding gift. It was one of her nightgowns, but she had never worn it. She had so many. Of course I was delighted with it and it fitted me in those days. *Ach*, but not for long! For three months it fitted me, then the children came and I got fat. But all these years I have kept it.'

'It is certainly worth keeping.' As I spoke a curious wave of relief went through me. There was nothing mysterious about the nightgown; it *was* Inga's. As I helped Charlotte with her toilet I felt ashamed of the vague suspicions which I had entertained. Ashamed, too, that I could feel such suspicion concerning a married man. Love, passion, jealousy . . . where would it all end?

The Count had already risen, as we discovered on going downstairs. I quickly caught the concern in his eyes as soon as he saw me. He asked me how I was and I replied that I was quite rested.

'Good. The mist is lifting; in another hour we should be able to leave for the schloss,' he said. The three of us breakfasted together; a simple meal of coffee and rye bread with fresh, unsalted butter. Inga left the room while we ate.

145

How strange it was to be breakfasting in such intimacy; to be pouring coffee for the Count. The sun shone through the mist and lit up the rather sombre room. It picked out the coppery tints in Charlotte's hair and the pale gold in her father's. The three of us talked together and it was very noticeable how much less nervous Charlotte was these days. Yes, I was bringing her out, I reflected. Undoubtedly my coming to Schloss Beissel had done her a great deal of good. As for myself . . . that was hard to say. However, when we finally arrived back at the schloss I thanked the Count for taking me to the hunting lodge and told him quite truthfully that I would not have missed it for anything.

I had a crumpled, tear-stained handkerchief as a souvenir of that trip. It bore the Count's monogram in one corner. I should have had it laundered and returned it to him. Instead I slipped it inside an envelope and put it in the dressing-table drawer.

The following day he left for

Karismette again and returned later in the week with the Countess. Not that I saw much of her when she was in the schloss, and when I did see her the same futile, unanswerable question would rise in my mind — why had the Count married her? However, one day she did visit the schoolroom, with unhappy consequences. Although Charlotte still wore a back-board every day, I had been giving her exercises to do for some time, and when her mother arrived she was walking about with a book balanced on her head.

'What are you doing with that book on your head, Charlotte?' asked the Countess angrily, looking at me as she was speaking.

'Charlotte is balancing a book on her head at my suggestion,' I said quickly. 'I am hoping she will be able to dispense with that back-board as soon as possible.'

'Are you, indeed?' the Countess was flushed with rage. 'How dare you interfere with my wishes in the schoolroom?'

Charlotte removed the book and stood looking from one to the other, her eyes wide with fright.

'I have not interfered with your wishes, Your Excellency,' I said. 'If you want your daughter to have a good carriage there are other ways to achieve it. I see no harm in what I am doing.'

'I am tired of your interfering ways!' she cried. 'You come here — trying to change everything — trying to impose your English ideas onto us — '

'Not at all,' I said, keeping my voice calm, although I could feel strong emotions rising. 'I have merely tried to introduce a little kindness and humanity into this schoolroom — into your daughter's life — '

'How dare you? How dare you say such a thing? You, a mere chit of an English governess — you dare to speak to me like that! I am a Countess! You don't imagine my daughter should be brought up as you yourself were? She is being brought up to take her place in society — '

148

'And how dare you speak to me like that?' My calm exterior had gone. 'You talk to me about being a Countess and about Charlotte taking her place in society. What kind of society, I wonder? From what I have seen and heard in this place — '

'Yes?' She was breathless with anger. 'What have you seen and heard?'

I glanced at Charlotte. She was white and trembling.

'I prefer not to say in front of Charlotte,' I said, recovering a degree of composure. I saw sudden fear in the Countess' eyes.

'Whatever you think is beneath my notice,' she said.

'Then why notice it?' I was completely reckless now. If the Countess dismissed me I would pack my bags and go. It would be the end of an intolerable situation, even though the very thought of leaving Schloss Beissel made my stomach churn with emotion. My adversary, however, seemed to have no answer to my last question. I suspected that she was incapable of carrying on a logical argument. I was grateful for the long hours I had spent in the Debating Society at school in Southsands.

'You will hear more of this,' she said in a low voice, open dislike blazing in her great amber eyes.

'Yes, and so will you.'

Her face now chalk-white, she left the schoolroom. Charlotte, not unnaturally, burst into tears.

'Don't cry, Charlotte,' I said, although I myself was trembling after the unpleasant scene. 'Whatever has happened, it has not been your fault.'

'But I don't want — don't want you to quarrel with Mama.'

Poor child, she was terribly torn. Her love for her mother was pulling one way and her affection for me, the other.

'I don't want to quarrel with her either,' I said. 'Cheer up, she may see things differently when she gives the matter more thought.'

I felt far from cheerful myself,

though. I had a feeling that whatever happened, I was going to have to leave the schloss. There was no place for me there now; no real happiness. Only this bitter-sweet tormenting love for another woman's husband, mixed with my disapproval of the whole way of life at Schloss Beissel.

I waited to hear more of the matter, as the Countess had warned me I would, but the days went by and no more was said. I taught Charlotte as usual; we carried on working in the garden together and I occasionally visited the Geisners in Goppertal. Then I realised that the Countess had decided to drop the matter, because I had made her think twice about it. She was afraid that I had seen something, or knew something. This would not make her want me to stay at the schloss, though. Far from it. Nevertheless, it meant that she would not risk a confrontation with me. My remark, spoken in anger, hinting at impropriety, had given me a curious hold over her.

Despite this, I felt under constant strain. The Count still visited the schoolroom, but as he never mentioned anything of the encounter between myself and his wife, I deduced that he knew nothing about it.

One evening when Charlotte returned from visiting her parents in the drawing room, she told me that her von Oldenburg cousins were coming for another stay, and that her father would be going hunting with Georg and the other men. I decided that I would not automatically accept that Frederica could join in Charlotte's lessons in the schoolroom as she had done earlier in the year. If the Countess expected that, then she could make me a formal request. Instead it was the Count who broached the subject in the schoolroom.

'You would be prepared to have Frederica in here with Charlotte again when her family visit?' he asked, shortly after his daughter had mentioned that they were coming.

'I do not think that the Countess is

very pleased with the way I conduct things in the schoolroom,' I said quietly.

He raised his eyebrows. 'Indeed? I had not heard so.' He glanced at his daughter who had flushed nervously and now sat at her desk, nibbling a pencil. It seemed to me that things were coming to a head. The tantalising nearness of his physical presence; the feeling that he visited the schoolroom mainly to see me and the sheer hopelessness of everything roused in me a mixture of longing, frustration and resentment.

'Charlotte, walk around the grounds for a few minutes. I wish to speak to *Fraulein* Burness in private,' he said. His daughter left the room immediately. I took a deep breath.

'What is wrong?' asked the Count. In the bright sunlight of early autumn the sabre scar on his face showed up distinctly. I fought down my emotions.

'I think,' I said, speaking with difficulty, 'I think perhaps it would be better for all concerned if I left the schloss.'

'Left the schloss?' The desolation on his face pierced my very heart.

'Miss Burness — ' he began to speak in his laboured English. 'Please do not think of such a thing. It would be so hard for Charlotte to bear, and my mother regards you highly. And — ' he broke off, floundering for words.

I decided to speak my mind. 'One of the reasons is because I feel a great deal of what I teach Charlotte will be wasted. I have been told in confidence by the Countess — your mother — that she is to marry your cousin Georg as soon as she is sixteen. I know that there are family reasons for this, and it is nothing to do with me. But I have had ample proof of the way he behaves towards women. If Charlotte were my daughter, I would not care for her to marry a man like that. And if that is to be her destiny, what need has she to be an accomplished woman?'

For a few moments the Count seemed to be completely taken aback by my forthright words. 'These are things which you do not understand,' he said at last. 'My cousin is perhaps a bit wild now, but he will settle down after he is married. That is another matter, though. What is this about the Countess not approving of your methods in the schoolroom?'

'For one thing, Charlotte is expected to wear a very uncomfortable backboard every day for several hours,' I said. 'I am giving her exercises in the hope that the need for it will soon be unnecessary. While she was doing one of these exercises the Countess came into the schoolroom and was angry about it. I have not seen her since.'

'She has said nothing to me about it. Occasionally the Countess has outbursts of anger, but she soon forgets them. The doctors say it is her nerves. I think she has been a bit overwrought lately. If that is all you are troubled about, then you should put it out of your mind altogether. There is no reason at all why Charlotte should not do these exercises if you consider them beneficial. It seems to me a fuss over nothing.'

'You may think so, Your Excellency,' I said in a low voice, 'but I do not think the Countess does.'

'I will speak to her about it. Meanwhile, you will agree to have Frederica in the schoolroom again?'

I could scarcely refuse. 'Very well. But it is still noticeable to me that the Countess has not come into the schoolroom herself lately.'

'Probably because she has been resting more than usual. The past few weeks have been rather taxing for her.'

They had been rather taxing for me, too, I reflected.

The Count appeared to think that he had been long enough in the school-room. 'I'll find Charlotte and tell her to come back now,' he said. At the door he paused for a moment, hesitating as if he had something more to say to me. Whatever it was, he must have thought better of it. He went out, closing the door quietly behind him.

I sat down, aware that I was trembling. I could not go on like this, I told myself desperately. The intensity of the feelings which his nearness always aroused frightened me.

A few minutes later the schoolroom door opened again and Charlotte stood there. Her childish face looked apprehensive and uncertain.

'Come on, Charlotte, let's continue with the lesson,' I said cheerfully. 'I expect we will be having Frederica in here, to keep you company.'

Instantly she brightened up and looked relieved.

6

The schloss was full of guests again, and the sound of voices and laughter echoed in the crisp autumn air. Rather to my surprise, the Countess had sent for me and asked me herself if I would mind having Frederica in the schoolroom again. Her manner had been detached, but not unpleasant. She had not mentioned a word about our differences. It was quite clear that the matter had been dropped and that she had decided that it was wiser to allow me to run things my own way. I was well aware that she had a motive for taking this attitude. It was not a situation that I cared for.

As for the Count, he seemed to have avoided coming to the schoolroom since that last visit. I did not think that he really approved of Georg as a husband for Charlotte, although he had implied that I had judged his cousin too harshly. Still, it was natural for him to want to think the best of his future son-in-law. So outwardly, since those few unbearably close, sweet moments at the hunting lodge when I had wept in his presence, life went on as usual, and the fact that I had another charge in my care made me too busy during the day to brood overmuch.

Again, the visiting von Oldenburgs had brought Baron von Schilsky with them. I learned that he was a superb shot and had stayed several times before. The children, including Charlotte, all called him 'Uncle Gustav' and he appeared to be popular with everyone. He was also an excellent card-player, a pastime which seemed to fascinate the von Oldenburg men, with the exception of the Count himself. He never joined in and I wondered if his brother's untimely end had anything to do with this. In contrast, Countess Maria adored all card games.

The main occupation was, however,

hunting. Looking picturesque in leather thigh boots, the men went into the forest for days at a time in search of their quarry, except on a Sunday, when nobody hunted.

I heard that another big ball was being planned for the house guests, and once again I was invited.

'You are going to the ball, *Fraulein* Burness?' the Dowager Countess enquired of me. How ill she looked; her condition appeared to be deteriorating rapidly.

'Yes, and Frederica and Charlotte are going for part of the evening,' I said. 'They are both very excited, needless to say.'

'Naturally. They are so young,' said Countess Adelaide sadly. 'I shall not be there.'

'I am sorry,' I said. 'Is that because you are not feeling very well?'

'Partly,' she said. I did not pursue the subject as I felt that it would have been impertinent.

I dressed carefully for that ball. Again I wore the very grand, cream-coloured gown which my aunt had bought me. Charlotte was in her white dress, her newly-washed hair glinting with coppery lights. No longer painfully thin, she appeared slender and graceful, and I caught a glimpse of the elegance and style which would one day be hers. She was just on the point of blossoming out, but what freedom would she have to enjoy her girlhood? None, as far as I could see, if she was to be married off so young.

Did freedom bring happiness, though? What happiness had it brought me? Not much up to now. Just the torment of being in love with a married man; the anguish of wanting to leave the schloss, and yet being unable to. It was as if the Count had put fetters on me.

It was with mixed feelings that I entered the beautiful *Rittersaal*. The musicians took their places and began to play. The early part of the ball was most enjoyable. Countess Maria was wearing a pale blue gown and looked extremely beautiful. When she led the dancing with her husband I caught sight of Baron von Schilsky's face. His eyes were fixed on her with open longing.

My own card was steadily being filled with names. Georg von Oldenburg approached me and stood before me, bowing mockingly. He asked if he might book a dance and I assented out of politeness. The Count also booked one, and later we waltzed together. Neither of us spoke as our bodies moved in unison. I did not feel as if I were dancing; it was more like floating. Within his arms I felt a mixture of sadness and joy; pain and happiness.

'Thank you, Miss Burness. That was . . . wonderful,' he said in English when the dance was over.

Much later in the evening, Georg claimed his dance with me. Charlotte and Frederica had been banished to bed and I realised that a good deal of drinking was going on. Nor was it confined to the men. There was the sound of high-pitched laughter and of loud female voices. The dancing went on and on. I knew by now that these balls had no official ending, but simply went on until everyone was exhausted.

'Are you tired, *Fraulein* Burness?' enquired Georg von Oldenburg, suddenly appearing beside me. His face was flushed and I could see that he was *weinfroh*.

'A little,' I replied, stifling a yawn. 'I seem to have been on the dance floor most of the evening.'

'Allow me to escort you to your room, then.'

'Thank you, but that will not be necessary.'

'So — you are afraid of my advances?' His voice was mocking.

'I am not in the least afraid, Sir.'

'You are very brave in company, I perceive. Not so brave when you were chosen to be the Rain Bird and I pursued you. I find you very attractive and rather different from the women I am accustomed to.'

'Really? From what I have heard, you

are accustomed to many types of women,' I said, rather unguardedly.

'*Ach*, so you have heard gossip? Well, that is not surprising. There is much to gossip about. In German society it is as well to turn a blind eye.'

'I am learning that,' I said quietly. As I spoke, Countess Maria danced past us with Baron von Schilsky partnering her. Georg chuckled as they went by.

'How Maria loves company at the schloss. These balls enable her to withstand the boredom of her existence in between.'

'If people are bored, they have only themselves to blame,' I said.

'Precisely. I am never bored. And I take it you yourself are never bored, being Charlotte's governess? You find her company congenial?'

'She is a very sweet child,' I replied, thinking as I spoke that she was far too good to become his wife.

'Not quite such a child now.' So he had noticed that the swan was beginning to emerge.

'No. She is growing up,' I said.

'You sound sad, *Fraulein* Burness. Do you feel sorry for Charlotte?'

'As you ask me, yes.' I was not prepared to enlarge on this.

'And Countess Maria, do you pity her also?'

'Why should I?' I countered.

'Do you then, perhaps, pity the Count?'

'You ask too many questions.'

Georg laughed and drank more wine. He urged me to have my glass refilled, but I declined. I noticed the Count glancing across at us.

'I myself sometimes feel sorry for Carl. He was a fine soldier, by all accounts. Perhaps it was just as well that he was wounded and had to resign from the army.'

'Why?' I asked, curious as always about the Count.

'Well, he would have had to resign in any case; he became the Count when his brother was shot in a duel, as you have probably heard. Schloss Beissel and the estates needed looking after. This schloss would have belonged to Otto, had he lived.'

I reflected that so too would the Countess Maria. Aloud, I remarked that I supposed it would one day belong to Charlotte.

'Yes, to Charlotte.' He spoke her name slowly, with a half-smile on his face. And to him, too, I thought.

'Do you not think the schloss is magnificent?' he went on.

'It is magnificently situated.'

'Is that all?'

'What must I say?'

'Well, do you not think it is beautiful?'

'Very beautiful. But in parts it is rather gloomy and I think the plumbing is terrible — '

He gave a shout of laughter. Just then Count von Oldenburg joined us and sat down on an empty chair beside his cousin. 'Are you still enjoying yourself, *Fraulein* Burness?' he enquired.

'You mean am I being a nuisance to

her?' asked Georg, with an impudent grin. 'She does not need your protection, Carl. She is most engagingly frank and direct. She does not think much of the plumbing in the schloss.'

I was most embarrassed at his repeating this. The Count looked mildly surprised. 'Is that true?' he asked me.

'I am afraid it is. I am surprised that the servants have all the trouble of bringing every drop of water into the house.'

He did not appear to have thought about this.

Georg was enormously amused. 'The Count is still a soldier at heart,' he said. 'He does not mind rising early; he does not mind if he has to wash in cold water. And if he had to live frugally and sleep on a trestle bed like a good soldier, he would not mind that either.'

'Perhaps not,' said the Count. 'However, had you been born at a different time, you might well have had to become a soldier yourself . . . I have often thought it is the greatest pity that you yourself have never had a taste of army life.'

'*Ach*, it is the greatest pity,' agreed Georg, laughing.

'Not that *Fraulein* Burness approves of soldiers,' went on the Count.

'Is that true?' enquired Georg.

'No — well, I mean, I used to enjoy the military balls that I attended at Leiknar, but I could not take the young officers as seriously as they took themselves — ' I broke off.

'You did not take them seriously?' asked Georg, leering.

'I think she means she could not take the profession of a soldier very seriously,' put in the Count. 'Is that not so?'

'Something like that,' I admitted. The three of us sat talking and Georg continued to drink heavily. His laughter grew more and more immoderate and, glancing round the room I was quite shocked to see several men slumped in chairs. I knew that the musicians continued playing until there was no further demand for them, and then they slept in any convenient spot. There was no sign of the Countess, nor of Gustav von Schilsky. Georg's buxom mother was dancing with his florid-faced, heavily-built father. They both had fixed, drunken smiles on their faces.

'Well, I must not neglect my other guests,' said the Count, looking round rather uneasily. 'I think a number of people have retired to bed.'

'I think that is probably a good idea,' I said. 'It has been a very pleasant evening. It was charming of you and the Countess to invite me.' I bade both the men goodnight, gave them a bow, gallantly returned by the two of them, and made my way out of the *Rittersaal*.

Just as I was leaving the room I gave a quick glance back. Instantly I regretted doing so. The Count and his cousin were no longer together, but I caught Georg von Oldenburg's eye and saw him rise from his seat. Knowing him, he could well interpret that backward glance as a discreet invitation. He knew that my bedroom overlooked the garden that we were busy in; the artless Charlotte had told him so. I felt that it would be prudent on my part to get there as soon as possible and lock the door.

There was a short cut, which entailed going near Countess Maria's chamber. I snatched up a candle, lit it and hurried along the corridors as fast as I could. How vast this place was, I thought. It had taken me weeks to get to know where all the corridors led and there were still parts where I had never been.

Suddenly someone appeared at the end of a passageway; a man in great haste. I stifled a cry, thinking that Georg had guessed I would hurry to my room and that he himself was rushing there, intending to make a nuisance of himself. It was not Georg, though. In the light of his candle I thought that I recognised Baron von Schilsky, although I only caught a quick glimpse before he disappeared.

I hurried along to my room and was

glad to close the door behind me and turn the key in the lock, just in case Georg followed me. The schloss was a creepy place at night; and what was von Schilsky doing, wandering around the corridors? That was hardly fair, though. He was probably going to his room, the same as I had been. But the direction he had been coming from was where Countess Maria's room was . . .

I prepared for bed. As I was sitting with my *peignoir* on, letting down my hair, I heard the sound of urgent footsteps and then a frantic banging on my door.

'*Fraulein* Burness! *Fraulein* Burness!' It was a woman's voice, distraught, hysterical. I hastily unlocked the door to behold Gertrud Krupp, trembling and terrified, an old wrapper flapping untidily around her and her scanty hair loose on her shoulders.

'Yes, what is it?' I asked, a nameless dread rushing through at the sight of her distress.

'Come quickly — it is murder!

Murder! *Ach*, it is terrible! Countess Maria has been shot dead! She is dead! Countess Maria! Shot dead — '

I was speechless. My numbed mind tried to take in what Gertrud was saying. The Countess shot! No, it could not be. I hurried out of my room, trying to calm the overwrought woman. I could hear the murmur of voices along the corridors; people were talking, exclaiming and weeping; all was confusion. The guests were carrying candles; some were in their night attire and some were still in evening dress. Gertrud, sobbing uncontrollably, led me through the open door of her mistress' room.

On the bed, clad in her blood-stained underwear, lay the beautiful Countess Maria. Her eyes were still open and her lovely hair was loose, covering the upper part of her body like a cape. She looked surprised. Stunned and ashen-faced, Count von Oldenburg was staring down at her, while sundry relatives tried to comfort him. A sheet was drawn hastily over the still form and the white linen showed dark crimson stains almost immediately.

'I found her shot!' screamed Gertrud. 'Shot dead!'

The room was packed with people. I noticed Georg von Oldenburg, now seemingly cold sober, standing with his father, silent and shocked.

'Murder!' cried Gertrud. 'Murder! Murder!' The poor, demented woman stumbled over to the bed and began clawing the sheet away from the body of the deceased Countess. It was horrifying; Georg and his father had to restrain her. The Count now appeared to recover some measure of composure.

'We must have the doctor from Goppertal immediately. And the police — ' he caught sight of me. 'Will you please do what you can to comfort Gertrud?'

'What about Charlotte?' I managed to say.

'She must not be told until it is absolutely necessary — ' he broke off. His agitation was so extreme that I wanted to turn away from it.

'And your mother, the Countess?'

'She must not be woken to be told this — in any case, she is having laudanum to help her sleep. Will you please take Gertrud away?'

'Very well,' I said quietly. 'Come, Gertrud.' I put my arms round the big woman's bowed shoulders and led her from the room. I had never cared for her very much, but her grief for her mistress was most moving. There was no doubt that she had been devoted to the Countess. I found that I myself was trembling uncontrollably. Gertrud's hoarse voice babbled on, almost incoherent at times.

'Some fiend must have got into the schloss unseen and murdered my mistress! Murdered her — ' she broke into a fresh spate of sobbing, as I guided her along to her own rather bare and comfortless room.

'I waited in her bedchamber as I always do when she is attending a late function. However late — always I help her to prepare for bed — but she came into the room and told me that I need not wait up for her any longer. She told me that she only wanted a handkerchief . . . ' Again the poor woman was overcome with grief. 'She said she was going back to dance, so I went to bed, although I couldn't sleep. About an hour later I wondered if she was back in her room, and if she needed any help to undress. I went to her room and the door was closed, so I knocked on it and there was no reply. Something made me open it, and there she was, lying on the floor in a pool of blood! Dead, *Fraulein* Burness! My little Maria — dead!'

She collapsed onto the bed, her sobs choking her. While one part of my mind was utterly stunned with the shock of what had happened, the other half remained quite practical.

'I'll get you some brandy,' I said.

'Murder!' screamed Gertrud again, her eyes starting out of her head. 'Murder! Murder!'

'Stay here. I'll be back in a moment,'

I said, and hurried away in search of some stimulant for the poor creature. Murder at Schloss Beissel! Was this all a nightmare; would I wake in the morning to find the autumn sunshine trying to break through the mist as usual, and everyone at the schloss getting over the revelry of the night before?

It was no dream, though. I took some brandy from the hand of a bewildered manservant. I could tell that he himself had been drinking; he knew that something had happened, but was not sure what. The whole schloss was in an uproar; I had my hands full with Gertrud and I dreaded anyone waking Charlotte and telling her what had happened. Avoiding everybody, I hurried back to that dreary room with its grief-stricken occupant.

I watched Gertrud gulp the burning liquid down, her eyes rolling wildly. I felt inadequate; I was sure that she needed a doctor. It was quite out of the question for me to leave her. Somehow

I got her into bed and sat beside her while she told me over and over again how she had left the Countess' room and gone back later.

Dawn was streaking the sky before she fell at last into an exhausted slumber. Her great, strong hands, those hands which could do such exquisite needlework, had been clutching mine. Slowly and carefully, I loosed her hold on me and rubbed my numb fingers. Sleep for me was out of the question for the remaining short time before Charlotte rose. Normally many people at the schloss slept late after a ball, but I knew that today that would not be so. Pulling my *peignoir* round me, I walked wearily along the corridors to my own room.

What was going on now in that large, beautiful chamber where the body of the Countess lay? The doctor would have been brought from Goppertal, and the police. It was all too awful to contemplate . . . Charlotte was now motherless. I crept into bed and lay shivering. Who had murdered the

Countess? How dreadful to have to break the news to her adoring parents in Karismette. Ahead lay the ordeal of the funeral ... my thoughts whirled round and round in my head. Despite the horror I felt, though, one thought came back again and again. The Count was no longer married.

The next few days passed in an unreal blur. Police in dark grey uniforms seemed to be everywhere, slowly and patiently questioning everyone; the servants, the guests and even the musicians. A bullet had been recovered from the Countess' body; it was established that she had been shot once in the chest at point-blank range, and that a pistol had been used.

The worst aspect as far as I was concerned was having to deal with Charlotte's grief. Her father had broken the news to her, but I had to take the brunt of the poor child's bewildered suffering. Even though the Countess had not been a very affectionate or understanding mother, still Charlotte had loved her. Frederica was subdued and weepy too; the whole atmosphere of the schloss had changed overnight. All around me were signs of grief; people talking in hushed voices, and the police gravely trying to find any sign or trace that might lead them to the killer.

None of the servants had seen anything untoward; none of them could help. There was much talk of the 'murder weapon'. A man named Max Jensen had been in charge of the gun-room at Schloss Beissel for twenty years, and his father before him. All the firearms were treated with great care. A record of every weapon was kept, and all huntsmen signed for any gun they took to use. As well as sporting guns, the gun room contained a wide range of antique armoury, including many pistols. The place was always securely locked when Jensen was not on duty. The police spent a long time questioning him, but no pistol had been removed. Jensen himself was a crack shot, and an expert on every type of gun. I heard later that he had broken down and wept at the way the Countess had died. Baffled and embarrassed, the police left him weeping in the gun room.

The walls of the castle were so thick that a pistol shot would not be heard except by someone standing just outside the room. And whoever had shot Countess Maria had made sure that there was no one about. Who would want to kill her, though? What motive would there be?

I had already been questioned by the police as a matter of routine. The inspector had asked me at what hour I had left the ball and gone to my room. I had replied that it was about two o'clock in the morning and that I had only been in my room about twenty minutes before *Fraulein* Krupp had banged on my door. The blue-eyed gentle-voiced inspector asked me if I had noticed anything suspicious; anything unusual. I replied that it had seemed much like the other ball which I had attended at the schloss; there were many guests; there was dancing, drinking and gaiety.

This was true enough. He did not ask me any more questions and I felt relieved. Nevertheless, the thought that I had not returned to my room by the usual route weighed heavily on my mind. Normally I never went near Countess Maria's chamber unless she sent for me. It was Charlotte who had shown me this alternative way to my room, adding that *Fraulein* Schiller had never used it, that probably it was not meant to be used by the governess. Nor would it have been, I reflected, except that from the *Rittersaal* I could reach my room more quickly that way. I had merely wanted to outwit Georg von Oldenburg in case he had tried to pursue me.

The fact remained that I had been in a part of the schloss where I was not supposed to be and I had seen the shadowy figure of a man, a man whom I had thought was Baron von Schilsky, but I could not be sure. I tried to dismiss the matter from my mind. There were so many other things to think about. I wondered how the poor Dowager Countess would be feeling, but she did not leave her room. The doctor was in constant attendance on her and Georg's mother was also unwell and needed medical attention. As for Gertrud, she appeared to be in a state of complete collapse and, almost without realising it at first, I seemed to assume a position of responsibility at the schloss.

I could not get the thought that I had seen Gustav von Schilsky near the Countess' room out of my mind, though. I remembered the stricken look on his face as he gazed down at the dead Countess. I pondered on what Gertrud had told me about how she had found her mistress shot. Had von Schilsky gone to the Countess' room and found her first? Suddenly I felt that I had to see him. Accordingly I despatched a note to him, asking him if he would come to the schoolroom shortly before *mittagessen* the following day. I said it was a private matter of some urgency.

No lessons were taking place, of course, although Charlotte and Frederica spent a good deal of time in the schoolroom with me. Some time before *mittagessen* the next day I suggested that a walk in the grounds would do them both good. Shortly after they had gone there was a knock at the door and I opened it, feeling extremely nervous.

Baron von Schilsky was standing there, dressed in black, but outwardly composed.

'Good day, Sir,' I said.

He inclined his head slightly. 'You wish to speak to me, *fraulein?*'

I caught a glimpse of the suffering in his eyes and for a moment I faltered in my intentions. 'If you can spare a few minutes, Your Excellency,' I murmured. He entered the room and I led him over to the fire, where I had placed two chairs. We sat down.

'It is concerning the night of the murder,' I said, and told him quietly that I had seen him in the vicinity of the

Countess Maria's room. 'You were hurrying along the corridor. I was going to my own bedroom and a short while afterwards Gertrud banged on my door in great distress.'

When I had finished speaking, he said in a low voice that if I told that to the police it would merely be my word against his. 'Nor would that prove anything, *fraulein*,' he added.

'Perhaps not, but there is more than that, Sir. I saw you earlier in the year, late one night, walking with the Countess. It was at the festival of the Rain Bird. I saw you embrace her. I think — '

'Yes? You think what?' His eyes, dark and disturbed, stared into mine.

'I think perhaps you were more than friends.'

'Do you? And what do you propose to do about it?'

'I just felt that I should tell you that you were seen once kissing the Countess, and that I saw you on the night of the murder.'

'And you think these two things are

very significant? You suspect me of foul play?'

'I did not say that.'

For a moment he did not speak. Then suddenly he began to weep. Sobs shook his frame. He covered his face with his hands and the tears ran through his fingers. 'I loved her,' he said, speaking with difficulty. 'Yes, it is true that I went to her room. I found her shot, but I dare not raise the alarm . . . it was dreadful . . . ' he broke off, unable to continue.

'Was she already dead?' I asked after a while.

'Yes, thank God. For what could I have done if she had not been? It would have been terrible, terrible!' The sight of his anguish was almost unbearable.

'And she loved you, too?' It was half-question, half-statement.

'Yes, she loved me, too,' came the muffled reply.

'What of the Count?' A strange mixture of bitterness and jealousy ran through me.

'She never loved him. She was compelled to marry him when she was little more than a child.'

'Compelled?'

'Yes. His brother had seduced her and she was expecting a child. Otto von Oldenburg was going to marry her because she was from a good family, too, and they weren't having any love child of the von Oldenburgs around the place. He should not have played fast and loose with a girl of his own class, and such a young one, too. Then, when he was killed, Carl did the right thing, for the honour of the von Oldenburgs, of course. He married her, but she was not consulted. He did not understand her nature — '

'Did she understand his?' I interposed, in spite of myself. 'I do not think it could have been very satisfactory for him.'

'But she was so lovely, so lovable, so sweet — ' he broke off and sobbed again. He had clearly been infatuated; he could see no wrong in her. But what he had told me was such a shock that I could scarcely take it in. So this was another secret of the schloss!

'Maria had been very spoilt,' he went on, wiping his eyes. 'Her family had adored her and indulged her. They didn't have her chaperoned properly; the poor child was taken advantage of. Her life had been ruined. At least, during the past year or so, I brought a little happiness into it.'

I felt dazed, taking in the full significance of what he had told me.

'So Charlotte is not the Count's child?' I said.

'No, she is his niece. But this is a secret, you understand, *fraulein*. Carl was a soldier when he married Maria, and she stayed at her parents' home to give birth to Charlotte. When the child was a few months old she came here to take up her position as mistress. Carl was the baby's father, to all intents and purposes.'

'I see,' I said. I felt drained of strength and unbelievably tired.

'I had better go now,' said Baron von Schilsky. He had regained a measure of composure. 'I shall be glad when the funeral is over and I can get away from here. God knows who killed Maria; he must be a fiend. Some madman is roaming about — if I could find him, if I could get my hands round his neck — ' he broke off and stood up. 'I dare not show too much emotion about Maria,' he explained. 'It has been a relief to tell you all this. Although you are young, I know that you can be trusted. I am glad we have been honest with each other.' He shook hands with me and left the schoolroom.

After he had gone I stood staring into the fire. The pine logs sent out their fragrance. I shivered in spite of the warmth. So many things had been revealed to me. I remembered the Dowager Countess talking about girls needing to be chaperoned. She had obviously never approved of Maria, but because she was expecting a child she had been obliged to accept her as a daughter-in-law. It had been a difficult situation all round; unsatisfactory for all concerned. Who had been to blame in the first place? It seemed to me that the chief culprit was the dead Otto. One could blame Maria, of course, but she had been a mere child at the time. Now I began to see why Charlotte had been the victim of such harsh discipline. The family were going to make sure that she did not bring any disgrace to the von Oldenburg name. Even so, I felt some indignation that the late Countess, having had so much freedom herself, was so strict with her daughter. Still, her freedom had brought her no happiness; motherhood at sixteen and a forced marriage. Baron von Schilsky had loved her, though, and it seemed that he had brought her some measure of joy over the past year or so.

But what of the Count? She had served him ill, and from what I had seen, he had tried to make her happy. Had he loved her? The old jealousy flared up in me. So Charlotte was really an orphan now. Yet there was no doubt that the Count cared for her as deeply as any father, and she adored him. He must have been about nineteen when she was born.

Charlotte and Frederica entered the schoolroom while I was thinking all this. How white poor Charlotte was. She was taking her mother's death very badly. And she and Frederica had enjoyed the ball so much. I was glad that she had her young cousin with her, otherwise the task of comforting her would have fallen the more heavily on me. I told the girls that I was going to see how Gertrud was. It occurred to me as I went along to her room that she must know all about Charlotte's true parentage.

Had she known of her mistress' relationship with Baron von Schilsky? Possibly, but if she had, she would keep such knowledge to herself. From what the Dowager Countess had said, Maria had pleaded ill-health to her husband when it had suited her. The Count had evidently not been near her room the night of the murder. She had kept him away, but she had encouraged her lover to visit her.

Poor Gertrud Krupp still seemed dazed by the tragedy. Although I had never liked her much, I felt pity for her now. She had taken care of the lovely Maria for the past thirty years, had dressed her and waited on her and loved her. Maria had been her life, and now, with Maria gone, her life had crumbled to pieces.

'*Ach, Fraulein* Burness,' she cried hoarsely when she saw me. 'Tell me, is this black cloak alright? I have had it some years. Is it alright to wear at the funeral?'

She was standing with an ugly black garment draped around her. She looked so ungainly and yet pathetic in it that I didn't quite know what to say for a moment. I finally told her that it seemed quite suitable.

'She is to be buried near the babies,' went on Gertrud. 'Near her three little boys. *Ach*, how I wept for her when they died.'

She began to reminisce about the happenings in her mistress' life, although I noticed that she never alluded to any of the events which I had learned from Gustav von Schilsky. She was indeed a woman to be trusted, as far as the late Countess was concerned.

'Somebody must have crept into the schloss and shot her for the sake of it. There is a murderer at large, *Fraulein* Burness, but the police will find him, be sure of that. He will suffer for this vile crime.'

'I sincerely hope they do find him,' I said. Later in the day the Count sent for me. How white-faced and weary he looked, and what lines of suffering there were on his face. He bade me sit down and I did so, as I had done at that earlier interview when I had been new to the schloss and full of ideas about changing things.

'First of all, *Fraulein* Burness, I must thank you for comforting my daughter during this time of great sadness,' he said. 'It has been dreadful; the schloss swarming with police and everyone in a state of shock about the whole terrible business. My wife is to be buried the day after tomorrow, as I expect you know. You will attend the funeral, I trust?'

'I will, Your Excellency,' I said. 'I will try to give Gertrud some support. Charlotte will have you and her grandmother.'

'My mother will not be attending the funeral. She is too ill — ' he broke off and twisted his hands together in a nervous gesture. I knew then that he was thinking it would not be long before the burial ground claimed her too. I remained silent, because I felt there was nothing I could say to comfort this man.

'The police have no clues — no suspicions, I suppose?' I said after a pause.

'Not yet. On such a night, with a ball being held and the servants being particularly busy, it would be comparatively easy for someone to enter the schloss unobserved. A stupid and motiveless crime — but there is no use going over it like this. What is done is done. Please continue to help Charlotte all you can — and poor Gertrud Krupp. Her life revolved round the Countess.'

'Yes, I know that,' I said. I longed to put out a hand and touch him. How much was he grieving for the Countess? I could not know that.

'It would help Charlotte if Frederica was allowed to stay a bit longer,' I suggested.

'I will mention it to her mother. I doubt if she will allow it. It is a good idea, though.'

A few minutes later I left his study, closing the door quietly behind me. I thought of how Baron von Schilsky had broken down and wept for Maria and told me of his love for her. Was the Count grieving as much beneath his controlled façade?

Preparations for the funeral went ahead and I could not help feeling that it would be a relief when it was all over. People from Goppertal climbed the mountain road with simple wreaths of autumn flowers and leaves woven into crosses.

The day Countess Maria was to be buried dawned clear and bright. A crisp autumn day, with the mountainside clothed in russet colours by the turning leaves. A day like any other, except that it was not. The funeral procession had to go down to the church in Goppertal for the service, and then back up the steep mountain road to lay the Countess to rest in the von Oldenburg burial ground.

Poor Gertrud Krupp sobbed uncontrollably in the church and so did Charlotte. The Count was very pale, but composed, and Gustav von Schilsky stared straight ahead of him, like a man in a dream. The lovely old church of St. Nicholaus was packed to the door. How much this was due to respect for the von Oldenburg family, and how much of it was curiosity because of Countess Maria's violent end was impossible to say. Maria's parents and family were there; the women almost foundering under black crêpe, and both her mother and father weeping openly. The whole atmosphere was charged with grief and drama. It was just as well that the Dowager Countess was not there.

The next part was even more harrowing; the long ascent back up the mountain road and the Pastor chanting the service over the open grave. It was close to those three little white crosses; as the coffin was lowered Maria's mother uttered a cry of anguish and would have fallen in a swoon if her weeping husband had not supported her.

Gertrud Krupp sank to her knees on the cold ground and began to pray. The Count stood with his arm round Charlotte. They looked so pitiful that I could scarcely bear to watch. Oh, for the whole business to be over and done with . . .

At last it was. People turned away from the graveside and walked over the rustling leaves, away from the burial ground. It seemed unbelievable that the Countess was no more. A week ago her little feet had been dancing and the arm of her lover had been around her. And now, what was left at the schloss?

Her husband was left, and her daughter; but Charlotte was not the Count's daughter. He had really nothing of his own to show for that marriage, I thought as we all entered the schloss again. In fact, all he had to show for his marriage, so dutifully entered into, were three little graves in the burial ground, and a fourth grave, newly dug.

7

I sat reading the latest letter from Alistair. It was loving and tender and after all the unhappiness at the schloss it was a relief to read of such homely and everyday things as he mentioned in it. Life at Southsands was going on in much the same way as it always had and somehow it gave me a feeling of security. Sitting with his letter in my hand I suddenly longed for the Downs, for England and home. This foreign castle was no place for me. If I returned to England I might find that my feelings for the Count were not as strong as I had thought. It was possible that I might find myself only too happy to settle down with Alistair and forget the echoing bells. Marriage was leading a life which fitted in with your husband's; my aunt had told me that often enough. And besides being dedicated to his profession, Alistair was so likeable, so attractive in every way . . .

Why was I trying to tell myself these things? My heart said no. This was love, this terrible consuming passion which I felt for a German Count. I put the letter back in the envelope.

Frederica's mother had not allowed her to stay at the schloss to keep Charlotte company. It seemed a bit uncharitable, but in a way I could not blame her. All the mourners had departed now, dressed in black and with sad faces. Even the high-spirited Georg had been subdued and serious on saying his farewells. The Dowager Countess had not left her apartments since the night of the murder; I had not seen her since before the shooting. I knew that she had not cared for Maria, but I had no doubt she would be filled with remorse now.

Charlotte and I put on our riding habits and we rode in the grounds of the schloss. The child was in very low spirits and nothing that I said seemed to interest her. Trying to cheer her up was an uphill task, as I did not feel very cheerful myself. Gertrud was another person who was leaning heavily upon me. She had now transferred all her attentions to Charlotte and she had a habit of breaking off whatever she was doing and weeping loudly for her dead mistress. I did not think this was doing Charlotte any good. As for the Count, he had kept very much to his study since the funeral. Altogether, life at the schloss was not very pleasant.

The police were still investigating the murder, and by now I had written home and told them of the tragedy, and how Charlotte had been left motherless. *Fraulein* Geisner had not yet appeared at the schloss to give Charlotte her music lesson. In view of what had happened, she was obviously waiting until she was sent for.

Charlotte was subdued and silent during our ride, and I felt relief when we were indoors again. It was cold outside, with a distinct nip in the air and the log fire in the schoolroom was welcoming. One of the maids brought a message from the Count, requesting both Charlotte and me to be in the drawing room before *nachtessen*.

'Gertrud will help you get ready,' I said cheerfully. 'It will be a good thing for your Papa to have some company.'

I took pains with my own toilet, changing out of my riding habit into a plain black dress. I felt it was only right that I should wear mourning for a time.

'Grandmama is very ill,' said Charlotte sadly, her eyes filling with tears. 'If she had felt well enough she would have sent for me by now.'

'Never mind, when she is feeling a little better she will,' I said. 'And you must try to be cheerful when she does.' I forced a smile. 'Come along, let us go and see your father.'

I had not seen him for a few days and I was glad he had sent for us. Since the departure of everyone from the schloss I'd had Charlotte all the time. It had been a strain and, as if that were not enough, I'd had Gertrud to comfort as well. Although I had not liked Countess Maria, her death had been a shock, and my personal feelings were very confused. I spent weary and sleepless nights.

When the Count greeted us in the drawing room I was shocked and concerned to see that he looked even worse than on the day after the shooting. His face was drawn and haggard, and there were dark circles beneath his eyes. He managed a wan smile.

'How are you, Charlotte? And you, *Fraulein* Burness?'

'We are getting back into a routine,' I replied cheerfully. 'I trust that the Countess is a little better?'

At the mention of his mother he looked grave again. 'She is not very well. The doctor is in daily attendance.'

'If there is anything I can do for her, please let me know,' I said.

'Thank you — at the present time there is nothing. She is not receiving anyone,' was his reply. He kissed Charlotte on her forehead. 'Grand-mama must rest all she can. Perhaps in a little while she will be strong enough to see you. I thought that the three of us might play one of your card games, Charlotte, and then afterwards we can have *nachtessen* together, if that is agreeable to you, *Fraulein* Burness.'

'Thank you. I think it will be a good thing for all of us,' I said.

Charlotte looked a bit happier. Poor child, it was only natural that she wanted to be near her father. Then the thought came to me that he was not her father really. That scarcely mattered, though, as far as their relationship was concerned. After playing several games of cards, the three of us had *nachtessen* together.

I could tell that the Count was making an effort to be cheerful for Charlotte's sake. I noticed that his hands were trembling and when he wasn't speaking his eyes seemed quite abstracted, as if only part of him was sitting at the table with us. He ate little and it seemed to me that the shock of his wife's death was affecting him more now than at the time.

'I think perhaps we should send word to *Frau* Geisner that she can come back and start Charlotte's music lessons again,' I said casually.

'That is a very good idea,' said the Count. 'Do what you think is best for Charlotte.'

'Might we go into Goppertal together and visit *Frau* Geisner's house, so that we can ask her personally to come back?' I asked.

'Well, if you think . . . ' he paused.

'It is a pleasant house,' I said hurriedly. 'They have young twin daughters there and the atmosphere is so happy. I think it would be good for Charlotte.'

'Then I have no objections.'

Charlotte looked pleased. Why shouldn't she go, I thought. The atmosphere at the schloss was such an unhappy one that it would do us both good to get away from it. I had begun to dread

Gertrud's daily visits to the new grave, and her loud lamentations afterwards.

In spite of the effort which I made to be cheerful, and the effort which the Count was obviously making, the evening passed slowly. My feelings were in a state of confusion; my emotions were so mixed that I could not have put them into words. I longed to know how much the Count was grieving for his wife, and how much of his distress was caused by the deterioration in his mother's health. He asked me to stay in the drawing room with him after Charlotte had gone to bed. With a shaking hand he poured out two glasses of wine.

'Don't think that I'm unappreciative of your help throughout this trying time,' he said quietly. 'My relatives have been very kind, but there are limits. And my wife's relatives are too distressed themselves to do much for anyone else. It was a relief when they went back to Karismette. I know it is not very pleasant for you at the present time.'

I sipped my wine. 'Under the circumstances, I can hardly expect it to be. I am trying to create a happier atmosphere, for Charlotte's sake.'

'I am aware of that. I am also aware how difficult that must be for you.'

I longed to reach out and press his hand and assure him that I wanted to help all I could. In fact, I longed to hold him close and give him comfort. At the same time I felt a strange jealousy that he could be grieving for such a worthless wife. He must have loved her, in spite of the fact that he had married her out of a sense of duty. She had been shallow, lacking in intellect, self-indulgent and spoilt. How could he have loved her? Yet I knew from my own experience that love was not to be commanded. I thought of that idyllic stay at the hunting lodge; of our shared happiness. I remembered the way the music had made me weep, and the soft glances which the Count had stolen at me. I had read more into these things than I should have. I stifled a sudden, involuntary yawn.

'You are tired, and no wonder,' said the Count.

'Yes, I'm afraid I've not been sleeping very well these past few nights.' I finished my wine. 'Will you please excuse me, Your Excellency? I would like to retire.'

'By all means. I hope you have a good night's rest.'

With a brief smile he bade me goodnight and I went thankfully to my room. Feeling completely exhausted, I tumbled into bed and fell asleep almost immediately.

The following morning I woke very early. It was just growing light. My throat was dry and parched. I rose and walked over to the washstand where I kept a glass of water. I had a few sips. To draw aside the curtain and peep through the narrow window was an almost instinctive act on my part. It was something which I did on waking every morning, although I knew that it was still very early, and that I would probably go to sleep again.

To my utter surprise, though, I beheld in the half-light the figure of a man approaching the gate of the derelict garden. The next moment I recognised it as being the Count. What was he doing out in the grounds as early as this? He wasn't strolling, but walking purposefully. The next moment I saw him stop by the old hawthorn tree. What was he doing? Whatever it was, he did not linger, but reappeared on the other side of the tree and then retraced his footsteps. He gave a quick glance round and then disappeared from sight.

Perplexed, I crept back into bed. I lay there, sleepless, thinking about what I had seen. What charm had the hawthorn tree that the Count would visit it so early in the morning — so early that even the servants were not yet stirring? I reflected that it was only by the merest chance that I had seen him; for all I knew he might have been walking round in this manner ever since his wife's death. A great desire rose in me to examine the hawthorn tree myself, nevertheless.

Accordingly, after lying in bed until it was a reasonable hour for rising, although still very early, I rose and made my toilet, washing in cold water, something which I was now accustomed to. I then left the castle and stepped outside into the chill of the early morning. My heart was thumping; suppose the Count was still wandering around? But if I waited until later in the day I would not have the opportunity to be in the garden alone. Pulling my thick cloak around me, I approached the hawthorn tree hurriedly, glancing in all directions. It looked to me as if he had been putting something in the hollow of the tree. I could have been mistaken, of course. It was all most mysterious. If he suddenly appeared, what would I say? He would think I had been spying on him. In a way, I suppose I had. No, that was not true. Anyway, what girl would not have gone and looked at the tree after seeing what I had?

Sheltered from view by the wall, I put my foot on the first two jutting branches and raised myself enough to peer into the hollow. Something was there. It was a small, brown paper parcel. I could not stop now. I reached down and unwrapped it, knowing that I had no business to, really.

The next moment I gave a gasp of horror. I was looking at a small pistol. It was beautifully decorated with silver and mother-of-pearl; I could see that it was an exquisite piece of workmanship. For a few moments I gazed at it in disbelief, then I hastily wrapped it up again and replaced it. I glanced fearfully round and hurried back into the schloss, up the stairs and into my room again. I sat down, my heart thumping painfully. The full significance of what I had discovered gradually came to me as I sat there.

Carl von Oldenburg had been out at dawn that day because he had wanted to conceal that weapon. The murder weapon . . . I knew that instinctively. I sat trembling, trying to work things out in my mind. He himself had murdered the Countess. The realisation hit me with a force that left me stunned. I had thought him badly wronged and deceived by his wife, but he had known what was going on and had taken his revenge. I tried to picture him opening her door and finding her partly undressed, preparing for her lover. Perhaps she had pleaded with him to spare her, but it had made no difference. My dear, beloved foreign Count was capable of shooting his wife in cold blood. I thought of him, tight-lipped at her funeral, comforting Charlotte. Oh, how little I really knew of these German aristocrats! They seemed to have their own code of behaviour about everything. But murder — that was something not to be lightly dismissed.

Why had he only just recently concealed the weapon, though? And why choose such an odd place to do so? Would he leave it there? It was all baffling, bewildering and, above all, frightening. What should I do about it? Tell the Count that I had seen him put something in the hollow tree and admit that I had looked and found a pistol? The idea had barely come to my mind before I dismissed it. I could not confront the Count with what I knew. It seemed to me that through no fault of my own beyond normal curiosity, I had stumbled upon something quite appalling.

He could not have killed her, I told myself. He would not do a thing like that. And yet, he had been a soldier, a dedicated killer. That was different, though; he had been fighting for his country. I stood up and caught sight of myself in the mirror. How tense and white I looked.

I drew in a deep breath. I would take Charlotte to visit *Frau* Geisner today and try and put the matter out of my mind for the time being. After all, strictly speaking, it was none of my business. I knew that was a ridiculous argument, though. A murder was everyone's business.

Forced cheerfulness seemed to be a way of life just now at the schloss. I wanted to try and lift poor Charlotte's spirits. Accordingly, even though it was an effort to drag my thoughts away from what I had found in the tree, I told Charlotte we would go to Goppertal that day. We set off in the carriage after *mittagessen*. For Charlotte to visit her music teacher would never have been permitted during her mother's lifetime. However, Count von Oldenburg seemed only too pleased to get the child away from the gloomy atmosphere of the schloss. At the last minute, Gertrud had one of her weeping attacks and it was with a sense of hearty relief that I sat in the carriage and was driven away from the castle.

We found *Frau* Geisner at home and, although Charlotte looked around her somewhat wonderingly, interest sparked in her eyes, which was a change from tears. The twins came romping home from school and she was shown their pet rabbits, the scrap books they were making and several other intriguing things. *Frau* Geisner made strong coffee and produced sticky cakes and talked incessantly in her comfortable, untidy sitting room. Emma was visiting an aunt, which was a slight disappointment to me, as her company was always welcome. However, talking to the jolly music teacher was a tremendous relief after the sadness of Schloss Beissel. She was very shocked by the shooting, although she said little in front of Charlotte.

'Such a pointless murder,' she remarked when the child was out of earshot. 'Motiveless.'

I nodded agreement, but the memory of what I had seen in the tree that morning came back to me. The Schloss Beissel murder was *not* motiveless.

Before we left the house *Frau* Geisner promised to give Charlotte a music lesson in two days' time. The visit had been a great success; my young charge looked much less forlorn, her cheeks were flushed and her eyes bright as she waved goodbye to the Geisner family. As we drove home, though, the thought of what I had discovered that morning came back to torment me. The carriage jolted up the steep mountain road; somehow I dreaded entering the schloss again.

Charlotte did not visit the drawing room to see her father before *nachtessen* that evening, as word came that he was not at home. Gertrud appeared, fussing round the child and weeping and wringing her hands until I felt infuriated. Sorry as I was for the woman, I knew that her presence in the schloss was not doing the girl any good.

As for the Dowager Countess, I knew that a nurse had been engaged to care for her. I felt that I would like to see her, but it was plain that the Count did not think it was a good idea at the present time.

Before darkness fell I managed to slip out into the garden. As I had done that

215

morning, I glanced fearfully round, but the place seemed deserted. Once again I put my foot on the projecting branch and eased myself up to look in the hollow. It was empty! I gave a gasp and stood down, my heart thudding. The evidence was removed. It had been done in a curious way, secretly, unhurriedly; it was all utterly mysterious and frightening.

I hastened back indoors, my mind trying to grapple with the situation. I almost tried to convince myself that I had actually dreamed that I had seen the Count there that morning; that I had never really gone there and discovered the weapon. But I knew only too well that it had not been a dream. The Count had murdered his wife, had somehow kept any suspicion away from himself, and had concealed that pistol. Why he had hidden it in the hollow tree that morning was a mystery, like so many things at the schloss.

He had disposed of it now, anyway. It was horrifying, unbelievable. This man whom I had loved with such a guilty passion, whom I had pitied because he was tied to the shallow, uncaring Maria, was a murderer. He had stood white-faced at the graveside, his head bowed, knowing that he had blood on his hands. The more I thought of it the more terrible it seemed.

8

I was in the middle of lessons with Charlotte when I next saw the Count. He strode into the schoolroom and it seemed to me that he was looking a bit less drawn in the face. It was two days after I had made the discovery of the pistol and I had thought of little else since.

In his usual courteous manner he asked how we both were, and I asked how his mother was.

'There can be no improvement,' he said quietly, clearly not wanting Charlotte to overhear.

'If I can be of any assistance — if you would not mind my seeing her — ' I suggested hesitantly, but he shook his head.

'Thank you, it is better not. There is a nurse in constant attendance. However, I should like to see you alone to discuss certain matters in connection with Charlotte and one or two other things.'

I felt rather surprised. At the same time the thought occurred to me that perhaps he was going to confide in me. But no, that was ridiculous. The feelings which his presence roused in me since I had discovered the murder weapon were just as tumultuous as before; but the intense love which I felt for him was mingled with the agonising feeling that he was not the man I had thought he was. My sympathies had been all with him; now they no longer were. I arranged to go to his study while *Frau* Geisner was giving Charlotte a music lesson. As I made my way through the corridors of the schloss to the Count's presence, my mind was a jumble of confused thoughts. Could I possibly challenge him with what I had seen?

I tapped on the door of his study and was told to enter. The Count rose when he saw me and offered me a chair opposite him on the other side of the fireplace. His manner was extremely nervous and I felt no less nervous myself.

After a few conventional remarks concerning Charlotte's well-being, and the possibility of her being allowed to see the Geisner twins again, the Count said that his real reason for wishing to see me was about a more personal matter.

'I have heard one or two things concerning your private life,' he said gravely. 'About your good uncle, the doctor and the young man who assists him. You are, I believe, friendly with the young man? I know that you write to him.'

'Yes, I write to him,' I said. I could feel my cheeks burning and my heart was thumping with a mixture of fear and excitement.

'Will you please tell me . . . are you intending to marry this young man?'

The directness of the question took me aback.

'Have you any particular reason for asking me that?' I managed to say.

'Yes. I wish to hear from your own lips that you are either engaged to be married, or free . . . ' he broke off. His face was white with emotion, although his voice was expressionless.

'There is nothing definite yet,' I said, as coolly as I could, adding that I did not understand why he was concerned about the matter.

'Do you not? Have you no idea at all that I hold you in very high regard? I know that the recent tragedy is still hanging over the schloss, and I am not asking you to make any sudden decisions; nothing like that. I would be willing to wait a year before — ' he broke off again.

'Before what?' I asked, and my voice came in a hoarse whisper.

'Asking you to be my wife,' he replied.

I sat rigidly in the chair, knowing that if I had not made that discovery in the tree I would have been extremely happy. I had dreamed of him saying those words, knowing in my heart that he never could. How I had yearned for the touch of his hand; had spent sleepless nights longing for this man. I could have him now, but at the price of my peace of mind. I saw clearly what I must do.

'I do not think you realise what you are saying. I believe the death of your wife has made you think you feel more affection for me than is the case,' I replied.

'You are entirely wrong if you think that, Marion. That is your name, is it not?'

'Yes, but my family and friends call me Marnie.'

'Marnie . . . *liebling* — ' he suddenly knelt down beside me. I was swept into his arms; at long last I felt his lips on mine and all my instincts urged me to respond, to press his face against mine and to lovingly stroke that flaxen hair of his. For a few brief moments I succumbed to the sweetness of that embrace; a sensation as strange and heady as drinking strong wine. He held me close to him, whispering endearments in German. How wonderful all this would have been if only I had not found a pistol in the hollow tree. I felt torn in two.

'Tell me that you feel as I do — I know you care,' he whispered. 'You came into my life like a breath of fresh air, like an English rose uprooted and put down in foreign soil. You are so different in your outlook from all the women I have known, so frank, so courageous, with the courage of your convictions. Always you see what needs doing and you make sure it gets done. If you think a thing is wrong, you will not endure it. And the way you walk — and the sweetness of your smile — oh, *liebling*, it has been torment for me sometimes, knowing that you were under the same roof and that I could not be with you — '

'Please! Let me go,' I said, trying to push him away. 'There are things I know, and other things which I don't know, but which I would like to have explained.'

'Things which you would like to know? What things?'

I was trembling violently. 'I happened to wake early one morning and I saw you putting something in the hollow tree,' I said.

The words had an immediate effect on him. He stiffened with shock.

'Yes, I was curious to know what it was,' I went on. 'I found out. You had concealed a small pistol there. It was the day I took Charlotte to visit *Frau* Geisner's house. That evening I went to look in the tree again. The pistol had gone. I believe it to be the murder weapon.'

He moved away from me and sat down in his chair again. The sweetness and intimacy of our embrace, the murmured words of love, seemed as if they had never been. All that was left was my flat, expressionless statement, which seemed to hang in the air while the Count sat without speaking.

'What do you propose to do about it?' he asked finally. All the tenderness had left his voice. I suddenly felt contempt for him.

'I don't know. I haven't decided.'

'There is really nothing you can do. You have no proof of anything; it is merely your word against mine.'

He had made no attempt to deny anything; he had made no excuse; no explanation. And I had wanted him to explain; I had wanted him to tell me why he had done what he had. Instead he had merely reminded me that it was my word against his if I went to the police.

'You admit it!' I cried. 'You sit there, knowing that I know of this terrible thing! And you actually talk about love — talk about making me your wife! Well, how do you feel, now that you know what I know about you?'

I was shaking from head to foot, and tears of deep emotion, of anger and disillusionment, began to run down my cheeks.

'I have admitted nothing,' he said quietly.

'But you don't deny it!' I cried. 'Tell me, did you shoot the Countess? Did you?'

'How dare you ask me such a question?' he said stiffly. The expression on his face was now one of arrogance and hauteur.

I stood up. 'How quickly you have changed.' I spoke tauntingly. 'You start off by asking me a personal question, but when I ask you one, it is all different. As you say, if I go to the police it will be my word against yours, nothing else. No other witnesses.'

He rose too. 'But you will not go to the police?'

My last illusion about him seemed to leave me. He had murdered his wife in a cowardly manner, and in an equally cowardly manner he was asking me to keep quiet about what I had seen.

'I hold you in complete contempt,' I said, suddenly regaining a measure of self-possession. 'No, I will not go to the police. I believe that people should be brought to justice for committing crimes, but I don't wish to be involved with anything further at this schloss. I sympathised with you deeply at one time — ' I broke off, thinking of his dead sons, of his seemingly loveless marriage and his faithless wife.

'You sympathised with me at one time,' he repeated, his voice harsh and strained. 'Why was that?'

'I felt that — that all was not well with your life,' I said, trying to fight down my emotions. 'I knew that your wife was . . . '

'Was what?' he almost hissed the words.

'Was not true to you,' I said at last.

His face was so set and white that it was like looking at a mask.

'I believe it is usual to say that the husband is always the last to find out these things,' he remarked after a pause. 'It is so easy to be deceived by someone whom you trust implicitly.'

'But that does not mean that you can

take the law into your own hands,' I said bitterly. 'From what I have heard, you have done many things in the past, with no regard for your own personal happiness, but just to protect the good name of the von Oldenburgs. Yet you commit a murder in cold blood; that shows scant regard for the family name.'

'You do not understand,' he said in a low voice. 'I cannot explain this thing.'

'No, you are right about that. But you do not deny doing it.'

He was silent.

'Deny it!' I cried, almost savagely. Again the tears streamed down my face. I longed for him to deny it; to give me some explanation that would satisfy me. I wanted with every breath of my being for him to say that it was not so, but the words did not come. Instead he stood looking at me, his eyes so desperately unhappy that I could scarcely bear to meet his gaze.

'I am leaving this place,' I said, as soon as I could trust myself to speak. 'If this is life as lived by the German aristocracy, I want no part in it. I've disliked a lot of ideas and a lot of things here right from the start. It's been an uphill battle to bring any joy into Charlotte's life. I don't envy her being a von Oldenburg; I pity her. Her life has been run on lines of military discipline and, like a soldier, she must do her duty — including marrying your cousin Georg. I am surprised that you are content to permit such a thing — but no — I am no longer surprised about anything about you — '

'Why should you think I am content that she should marry Georg?' he interrupted harshly. 'He is not all that I would wish for her, but it is something we must make the best of. He is my cousin's oldest son; it is only right that he and Charlotte should make a match of it. He is a von Oldenburg; what else can we do but marry Charlotte off to him?'

'You can let her have the right to some freedom,' I said passionately. 'You have robbed her of her mother — and whatever she was, Charlotte loved her. I am fond of Charlotte and care for her welfare, but I am going back to England now. I have had enough. I shall be sorry to leave the poor child.'

'Leave her! But you can't leave her — you can't go back to England and leave her with no woman to turn to! My mother is dying — '

'Yes,' I said sadly. 'It is a sorrow to me. There is not much happiness in this place at all. The best thing for Charlotte would be to become a pupil at my old school near Leiknar. She would receive both kindness and companionship there.'

'I ask you to stay, for her sake,' he said earnestly. 'Not for my sake — you may think what you will of me — but for Charlotte's sake. She needs a woman's guidance, now more than ever. I entreat you to stay.'

'I am sorry,' I replied firmly, 'but my mind is made up. There is nothing you can do to persuade me to remain here.'

'But you would have stayed if you

had not seen me in the garden early one morning?'

'Yes, I would have stayed. But I have accused you of your wife's murder and you have not denied it. You surely do not imagine that I could live here under such circumstances?'

'And you can go — walk out — without it meaning anything to you?'

'I cannot stay,' I repeated. 'You need not be alarmed; I shall not mention to anyone what I have seen here. I shall return to England and try to forget.'

'Forget — ' he began, then stopped himself. 'You will marry that young man you write to?' It was partly a question, partly a statement.

'What I do is scarcely any concern of yours,' I said icily, and left the room without a backward glance.

My legs felt weak and I was trembling uncontrollably. I wanted to go somewhere and sit down for a while. I went to my room, closed the door behind me and sank down onto the bed. The shock of finding the pistol was, in a way, less shattering than the shock of accusing the Count of being a murderer, and of him not denying it. Oh, the passion of those hungry kisses! My aching heart cried out to him, and yet, how could I love a murderer? It was all too terrible. He had talked of making me his wife, and if I had not seen what I had, how different every-thing would have been. He would not have been any less guilty, but I would not have known. I lay on the bed, tears of grief and disillusionment coursing down my cheeks. And another thought came to me, so horrifying that I wanted to shut it out of my mind. But it came back, persistently, remorselessly.

There was no mistaking the passion he felt for me. He had told me it had been a torment for him knowing that I was under the same roof, and yet being unable to tell me of his love. Was it possible that he had murdered Maria, not because she had a lover, but because he wanted the way to be clear to marry me? No, it could not be; it was too horrible to contemplate. The shock went through me to my very bones.

A man had murdered his wife so that he could have me. My intense feelings for Carl von Oldenburg, feelings which had become a part of my life, were replaced by a sense of revulsion. I had been quite mad to have cared for such a man. The sooner I left Schloss Beissel the better. My uncle had mentioned in his last letter that my aunt had not been so well lately, so if they were surprised at home when I left the schloss so suddenly, I would merely say that I thought I should be with Aunt Matilda if her health was below par.

I doubted if they would question my decision overmuch, though. My aunt would not wish me to stay in a place where there had been a murder, and I didn't think my uncle would either. As for Alistair, he would certainly be pleased to see me back in England.

Charlotte . . . yes, it was hard on the child. It would be an awful wrench to leave her. I tried to think of the Count with detachment. Caring for him had been a foolish dream, mixed up with the enchantment of living in a real German schloss and of meeting a real German Count. Of course, I had imagined myself in love with him, it was all part of the fairytale. I had a sudden longing to get away from that place and to wake again in my own familiar room at Southsands. There was also a sense of relief that I had decided on a positive form of action. After all, it was my life that was important to me, and there no longer seemed to be anything to tie me to the schloss. It was hard on Charlotte, but she was not my responsibility. I had done my best for the child.

I glanced at my watch and realised that I had been in my room for nearly an hour, pondering on my situation. I rose from the bed, combed my hair and removed all traces of weeping from my face. I still looked very pale, though. I pinched some colour into my cheeks before making my way to the school-room.

Frau Geisner and Charlotte both greeted me warmly and we took coffee and cakes together. I found myself smiling and talking and behaving as if nothing had happened. Charlotte looked happier than she had done since her mother's death, and I knew that it was not going to be easy to tell the poor child that I was returning to England. I thought of the Count's mother. Every time I had suggested that I would like to see her, he had refused to allow me to. I could not flout his wishes in that respect, but at least I would write a kind note for her before I left the schloss.

So I made my plans, even as I was laughing and talking with *Frau* Geisner and Charlotte. Back in England, all this would seem like a dream. The draughty corridors; the primitive plumbing; the sound of German voices. The mountainside with its echoing bells, — yes, that would seem a dream, too; so would a bright-haired girl who had turned to me in her loneliness. And a man whom I had first seen riding a black horse and looking like a Viking god, would he seem a dream, too? A man with a scar on his face and hand; an aristocrat and a soldier in the true tradition of his race?

I had loved him. Loved him! And he had murdered, for love of me.

As I put down my coffee cup a maid entered the schoolroom, bearing a silver salver in her hand.

'A telegram for *Fraulein* Burness,' she announced and left the room.

Frau Geisner and Charlotte watched me silently as I opened the envelope.

'It's from my uncle,' I said, trying to fight back a feeling of faintness.

'My aunt is ill. She's had a heart attack. I must go home at once — at once —'

'She's fainting,' came *Frau* Geisner's voice from a long way off. 'Ring the bell for help, *liebling*. She has had too much strain lately.'

9

'Thank heavens,' said my uncle quietly, the day after my aunt's funeral, 'thank heavens you got back here in time to see Matilda alive. It must have been Providence.'

His words brought back vividly the painful memory of my departure from the schloss. I did not want to remember it. Too many other things had happened since then, anyway. My aunt had had another heart attack while I had been travelling home and she had only lived until two weeks after Christmas. It was not a very happy beginning for the new year. The nursing I had had to do and the daily strain of seeing her gradually growing weaker had been a terrible emotional and physical ordeal.

I had been plunged straight from the bitterly unhappy atmosphere of the schloss into an atmosphere of sickness and worry at home. There had been no mistaking the warmth and delight of my uncle's greeting; he was glad I had come home, and certainly Alistair was pleased. The first time he had tried to embrace me after my return I had felt myself stiffen in his arms. He had immediately sensed that I was tensed up, and remarked with his usual kindly patience that it was only natural that I was upset about things. He was fond of my aunt, and I was deeply touched to see how concerned he was about her condition, and how he took the burden off my uncle at every opportunity.

When the end came it was very sudden and the shock was a stunning blow. My aunt's sister, Alice, was laid low with an attack of influenza and was unable to attend the funeral. This was a relief in a way. I thought of Aunt Matilda constantly; I realised now how dear she had been to me, with her kind, fussy ways and her desire for me to settle down with Alistair. It was a bitterly cold winter afternoon and I sat in my black dress in the drawing room with my uncle and rang the bell for tea.

I observed with a feeling of sadness how much older he looked. I felt remorse that I had ever gone to Germany. I should have stayed at home and done my duty by my aunt. For, after all, what had I gained by going to Schloss Beissel? Nothing but heartache. And now, what plans had I for the future? The tears stung my eyes. Everything seemed so futile, somehow. I felt older by years and years than when I had attended Miss Hetherington's school, and yet, it had not been all that long ago. The high-spirited debates and the many discussions which we'd had together had all been theory. I knew that now.

'Alistair should be calling round before long,' remarked my uncle as I poured the tea. 'I don't know what we would have done without him. Matilda was very fond of him.'

'Yes, I know,' I said hastily. I felt that I knew the lines on which my uncle was thinking and, although I understood how he felt, I could no longer fit in with what he wanted. It would be the most natural thing in the world, after a period of mourning, for Alistair and me to announce our engagement. Then we could marry and I would settle down in Southsands, just as my aunt had hoped I would.

But if I didn't marry Alistair, what then? My rosy dream of a somehow different and exciting future would still remain unrealised. Going to Schloss Beissel had been my big adventure and it had ended with sadness and disillusionment. Anyway, I could not think of leaving my uncle alone and going away again. I poured some more tea for him.

'He's a very fine young man,' he said thoughtfully, sipping it. 'I think I shall make him a partner here as soon as possible.'

'That is up to you, Uncle,' I said. He gave me a quick glance.

'I know things have been difficult here lately, Marnie, and you haven't had much time to think of yourself, but you are young and you want a young life. I mean — well, you and Alistair — ' he broke off, having said just enough to imply that he would not expect me to remain single and look after him for the rest of my life.

'As you say, Uncle, things have been difficult lately. I have no particular plans for the future.'

'But your aunt was sure that you and Alistair . . . ' he paused. 'He talked of you constantly while you were away. Your aunt and I both thought that when you came back from Germany for good you would be making wedding plans.'

'Well, don't try to rush me into anything,' I said, attempting to speak lightly, although I had a heavy enough heart. 'It will take some time to get over Aunt Matilda's death.'

'Indeed it will.' We talked of other things then; trivial, everyday things, but I knew that my uncle sorely missed his wife's presence in the house, and I felt shattered sitting there, knowing that never again would I see her plump little hands pouring out the tea, or have her fuss lovingly over me. The arrival of Alistair interrupted our melancholy *tête-à-tête*.

'I shall be attending to my patients as usual tomorrow,' my uncle told him.

'There is no need. You have been under considerable strain lately,' Alistair said. 'Tell your uncle he is to rest for the remainder of the week, Marnie. And you need a good rest, too.' I caught the look of tender concern in his eyes.

'Yes, you are right about Marnie,' said Uncle Peter. 'She's been doing far too much ever since she came home. She had already been tired out at that schloss. We don't want any more sickness in the house.'

I rang for more tea, and Alistair sat and talked quietly to us both. I could see how his gaze lingered on me and I knew that, now that my poor aunt was no more, he would feel free to plan for the future. With a sense of panic I realised that he might try to get a definite understanding between us.

'Well,' said my uncle after we had talked for some time about quite general matters, 'if you two will excuse me, there are some papers I must look through in the study.'

He discreetly left the room and, as soon as the door closed behind him, Alistair rose and came across to me. His arm went protectively around me.

'Your uncle is making an effort to get back to normal,' he remarked. 'I'll see he doesn't do too much for the next few weeks.'

'You are kind, Alistair,' I said, and meant it. He squeezed my shoulder lovingly and kissed me.

'I've not had much opportunity for this sort of thing,' he said. 'It's been rough for you lately, Marnie. You've tired yourself out caring for your aunt and that murder at the German castle must have been a terrible shock for you. Believe me, I understand how you must feel.'

Do you? I thought bitterly. I scarcely understood myself, so confused were my thoughts.

'I don't want you to feel that I'm rushing you or anything like that, dear, but you must know that I would like us to become engaged. Your aunt went so far as to talk to me about it while you were in Germany.'

'I expect she did,' I said. 'She was very fond of you.'

'And of you, Marnie. She told me that she knew she could trust me with your happiness and you must know it's true. I know you've had a trying time lately, so I don't want to seem too demanding, but I would like to hear you say that you care for me, and that we will be getting married as soon as possible.'

'But Alistair, you *are* rushing me,' I said, fending for time. My uncle's words came back to me and I thought how ironically true they were. He had said that I could go farther and fare worse. That was precisely what I had done . . .

'I'm sorry,' said Alistair. 'It's not the time to talk about such things. Kiss me and tell me that you still care.'

'Of course I still care,' I murmured, pressing his hand. I kissed him, as he had requested and, although it was pleasant and satisfying, there was none of the anguished passion I had felt in my only embrace with Carl von Oldenburg. What was I to do? If I married Alistair, would I settle down and be happy, and would those vivid, painful memories of Schloss Beissel and all its occupants gradually fade? I suddenly began to weep, and Alistair drew me onto his knee and comforted me.

'It's all been too much for you,' he murmured, kissing my hair. 'And I've been thoughtless, trying to get you to make plans while you are feeling so upset about your aunt. I should realise that you are back home now and you won't be wanting to go off to Germany again.'

'No, I won't be wanting to do that.'

We sat in silence for a while. I don't know what Alistair was thinking, but I was thinking that circumstances seemed to be taking charge of my life instead of the other way round. Looking after my uncle was now my obvious duty. He held Alistair Harlow in high esteem; there was no doubt that he would readily give his blessing to a marriage between us.

By the end of the next fortnight life had returned to some sort of normality. I endeavoured to take my aunt's place as much as possible and tried to ensure that the household ran smoothly. I had not had time since returning home to have any social life, and I was rather surprised one afternoon when Tina announced that there was a young lady to see me. She added that the lady would not give her name.

I was in the drawing room and the next moment Isabel Fairclose appeared, looking absolutely radiant in a wine-coloured coat, with a little matching forward-tipped hat and a grey squirrel cape and muff. Her figure had slimmed down to fashionable elegance, so that she did justice to her expensive clothes.

'Marnie! How lovely to see you again! I wanted to surprise you. I haven't written, I know, because I'm not much of a letter-writer — '

We embraced and she sat down. 'Papa has retired and we've just moved into a house at Southsands. My parents always liked it here, you know. I've heard that you've recently lost your aunt. I'm so sorry.' Isabel's brown eyes were sympathetic. 'What will you do now? You've had a position as a governess in Germany, haven't you?'

'Yes. I suppose I will look after my uncle now.'

'Your uncle is nice — ' she broke off as Tina tapped at the door again and announced Miss Hetherington. I had only seen her once, very briefly, since my return from Germany and she advanced into the room smiling, with her hands outstretched.

'Marion, how are you? Isabel, what a

surprise to see you, too! Well, I'm meeting two former pupils instead of just one as I had expected.'

The warmth of her personality seemed to fill the drawing room and we both smiled, feeling very young again under her benign influence. Isabel talked about her travels in Italy the year before and what a charming house her parents had bought at Southsands.

'So Marnie and I will be seeing quite a lot of each other,' she finished.

Miss Hetherington then turned her attention to me. She said she had come partly to offer her condolences and partly because she had a proposition to make.

'Miss Schwele, our German mistress, is leaving us for a while. Her father is very ill, so she has gone back to Germany. I am quite sure that you could help us out teaching German, Marion. It would not take up all your time, but you would be busy enough mentally not to have too much time to grieve. I would be grateful if you would think it over and let me know as soon as possible. Your German was always excellent and it must be quite perfect now.'

For a moment I was too surprised to reply. Also I was battling with unexpected emotions which had suddenly risen in me at the thought of once again speaking German.

'Well, I said think it over,' continued Miss Hetherington. 'And how is your uncle?'

The words were no sooner out of her mouth than he appeared at the door.

'Why, Miss Hetherington. And Isabel! What a lovely surprise.'

He shook hands with them both, genuine pleasure on his face. Miss Hetherington had called at the house once before since I had returned from Germany, but only for a few minutes, knowing how ill my aunt was. She had probably heard about the tragedy at Schloss Beissel from my uncle, but she was too tactful to mention it.

'We are having a reunion, Uncle,' I

said. 'Isabel's father has retired and they have bought a house in South-sands and are living here. Isabel came to see me as soon as she could, and then Miss Hetherington arrived.'

'I've just been telling your niece that I've come with a proposition for her,' said Miss Hetherington, beaming.

'Not another position in Germany, I hope,' was my uncle's immediate reaction.

'Indeed, no. I'm offering her a temporary position at the school, teaching German while our Miss Schwele is away. What do you think of the idea?'

'I think it is a splendid idea,' said Uncle Peter. His eyes met mine. 'But of course, it's for Marnie to decide. As you know, she's had a trying time lately and she may not feel like tackling it.'

'I think I would like to try,' I said.

'I knew you would.' Miss Hetherington looked delighted.

I rang the bell for tea and the next hour passed very pleasantly. My uncle had always liked Miss Hetherington and he seemed pleased that she had called at the house so informally, without a visiting card, in much the same way as Isabel had. We were certainly having an unexpectedly lively afternoon. Our next visitor was Alistair, who looked rather surprised to find us entertaining two ladies. He knew Miss Hetherington, but not, of course, Isabel.

'Isabel and I are old school friends,' I explained as I introduced her. 'Her father has retired and now they have settled in Southsands.' Isabel dimpled delightfully in his direction.

'We will be seeing more of you — and of your parents, I expect,' remarked my uncle.

'Not professionally, I hope,' said Isabel with another smile.

'I hope not either,' said my uncle. 'I know your father is a keen golfer, so I expect he will be joining our club.'

The unexpected company cheered and relaxed me amazingly and I could see it was having the same effect on Uncle Peter. Alistair kept glancing at me tenderly. I felt that if I took this position at my old school it might be the very thing to get me out of this sense of being stifled; of having walls closing in on me. For the first time since my return to England I was being offered some mental stimulation. And if I were busy teaching and running the household for my uncle, I would simply not have the time for brooding about things.

After dinner that evening, Uncle Peter and I sat talking.

'You should take that position Miss Hetherington offered you, Marnie,' he said. He lit his pipe. He no longer went to his study to smoke; I had told him that I did not object to pipe smoke. My aunt had always hated it.

He sat back in his chair. 'You'll have young companionship and plenty to occupy your mind. Miss Hetherington is a splendid person and I'm very pleased that your friend Isabel has come to live in Southsands. She is a charming girl and I like her parents.'

'Never mind about my life,' I said. 'What about your life? You've had no social life at all for months. You mentioned golf — does that mean you are going to take it up again when the weather improves a bit?'

'Yes, I think I should. One cannot live in the past, however much one wants to. Life must go on.'

When he said that I thought straight away of my own past; a past quite recent, but one which I would be happier to forget. It would be a challenge to teach again, but this time I would not be teaching English, but German; *his* language. Looking into the cheerful coal fire I seemed to see another fire, made of fragrant pine logs. I seemed to see a pale, proud face; *his* face, with its livid scar over the cheekbone . . . his blue eyes and the anguish in them when I had said that I was leaving the schloss. Painful memories crowded in on me. The sound of his voice speaking his native language with elegance and authority. The sound of his voice speaking English, fumbling endearingly for the right word . . .

My uncle leaned forward unexpectedly and patted my hand. 'A penny for them, Marnie.'

'I was just thinking about Germany,' I said, in some confusion.

'Are you missing it?'

'Missing it? Oh, no. I've lived there and I know what it's like.'

'You haven't talked about it much at all.'

'No. It ended unhappily. I was going to leave in any case — even before I got your telegram.' As I spoke I remembered the sound of Charlotte's sobbing when I had told her that I was leaving. If only I could blot out these anguished recollections.

'Were the von Oldenburgs a nice family?' asked my uncle.

I shrugged. 'Well, they had some strange ways. They were real German aristocrats. Charlotte, the daughter, was a sweet child; I was very fond of her and I think she was of me, but her upbringing had been very strict. There were many things I did not approve of.'

'Ah,' said Uncle Peter sagely, nodding his head. 'Did you try out any reforms?'

In spite of the unhappiness of remembering, I could not help smiling. He knew me so well.

'I suppose I did. I told them that I didn't think Charlotte got a good enough diet. She was only allowed thick milk for supper and cakes were considered treats that she could rarely indulge in. I told the Count and Countess what I had for supper at Charlotte's age.'

'Bread and dripping, if I remember rightly,' said my uncle with a chuckle.

'Yes, that's what I told them.'

'And what happened?'

'The Count hadn't known that Charlotte only got milk for supper. He said she had to have something more substantial. Oh, there were a great number of things I disapproved of.'

'And you battled to have them changed?'

'Yes, I suppose I did. And I got quite a number of them changed, too. The Countess was not always pleased . . . ' I broke off, remembering her petulant ways; Baron von Schilsky who had loved her, and her terrible end.

'Didn't you get on with her very well?'

'No, not really. I didn't approve of a lot of things about her. I liked the Dowager Countess.'

'And the Count?'

'He was very proud of being a von Oldenburg,' I said. 'He had been a soldier and had fought in the Franco-Prussian war. He had been invalided out with a hand wound. I don't think he ever got over having to leave the army. Everything he did seemed to be with the honour of the von Oldenburg family in mind. And Charlotte seemed subject to almost military discipline — and I didn't approve of the fact that she was to marry a distant cousin as soon as she was sixteen. Georg von Oldenburg is about twenty-five and a terrible rake. Charlotte is much too nice for him — '

I broke off, surprised that all this had come out in a flood to my uncle. Up to now I had said very little about my experiences at the schloss. Yet this torrent of bitterness now poured out.

'And did you say that she was too nice for him?'

'As a matter of fact, I did. But I had already made up my mind to leave the schloss then.'

'And the tragedy of the shooting? You wrote and told us about it, but you haven't enlarged on it at all since you returned. Of course, I know there have been other things to think about.'

'I don't like to think about it. It was a dreadful business.'

'The Countess was shot during a ball wasn't she?' My uncle puffed thoughtfully at his pipe. 'It sounds a rum business to me. You said in your letter that the police thought someone had entered the schloss and escaped again before the crime was discovered. In spite of that, to me it sounds more likely to have been done by someone inside the schloss. Of course, I dearly love a mystery, as you know.'

I laughed, but it was a forced laugh. 'Yes, you always did. It's rather different when one is actually there and something like that happens.'

What would he think of it all if I told him the whole truth? If I told him about the murder weapon which I had found in the hollow tree? And of the motive behind the murder? I gave an involuntary shudder, remembering my poignant accusation of the Count and how he had refused to deny it, seemingly being only concerned that I would not tell the police what I had seen . . .

I became aware that my uncle was speaking again. 'What will happen to the daughter, then? It is sad for the child with no mother.'

'Yes, it is sad,' I agreed. 'I suggested

that she should go to the *Damenstift*.'

'The child — Charlotte — will not be writing to you, then?'

'No. I thought it better not to.'

For some time there was silence in the room. Uncle Peter sat smoking, staring into the fire and I sat nervously twisting my handkerchief, thinking painful thoughts of the past.

'Well, my dear, I expect it was an experience for you,' said my uncle finally. 'It must have given you an insight into the way of life in these remote German castles.'

'Yes,' I said. 'It certainly did that.'

For a few minutes we seemed extremely close. He reached out and gave my hand a little squeeze. It almost seemed as if he understood that I had been very unhappy there without being told. When I went to bed sleep was impossible. I lay, turning this way and that, thinking of my lost love, wondering what had become of Charlotte and how the poor Dowager Countess was. It was morning before I fell into a doze, but when I woke I had reached a decision.

Looking at my somewhat pale face while I was making my toilet, I made a fierce resolution that I would throw myself into life at Southsands and not spend a moment brooding over what had gone, nor would I sit and grieve about my aunt. The past was the past. I would take up the position offered me by Miss Hetherington and I would not be rushed into anything binding concerning myself and Alistair for the time being. In fact, I would live each day as it came and put into it as much as I was able.

Having made this resolution, I found renewed strength. I went to Miss Hetherington's house and told her that I would take up the position as soon as she needed me. Alistair seemed to think that this was a good decision on my part, 'for the present time', he added. He had said no more about our getting engaged. Clearly, he was biding his time. Meanwhile we continued to see a good deal of each other.

10

The winter went by and slowly the days turned into spring. I was working as hard as I had planned, but life was not all work. I had joined a musical appreciation society in Southsands which I attended with Isabel, and recently Alistair had joined it, too. Miss Hetherington was utterly charming to me, and I found an unexpected satisfaction in teaching German to the girls at her school. It was ironic that, although I wanted to put the past behind me, I was constantly using German words and phrases.

There were times when I would hear a young girl speaking and suddenly I was transported far away and was sitting in a shabby schoolroom, listening to Charlotte. And then the door would open and a tall, fair-haired man would be standing there watching. A man who had loved me — loved me! But a man who had murdered for me . . . this was the point at which I always came down to earth and the dream would fade.

Miss Hetherington began to come to our house more and more frequently. I thought at first that she came because she felt sorry for me, and also because she liked to discuss school matters with me now that I was teaching there. She had asked me to take an active part in the Debating Society, and I found that another interest.

She came one evening and I could not help thinking how nice she looked. She was tall and carried herself very well and, although, of course, she was no longer young, she had fine eyes and her grey hair was beautifully dressed. She was wearing a very becoming blue coat and hat and I saw the pleasure on my uncle's face when he greeted her. He mentioned that there was a particularly good play at the Theatre Royal the following week and suggested that he and Miss Hetherington should make up a foursome with Alistair and myself and see it. Everyone was agreeable and we had a most enjoyable evening. The theatre was well attended and afterwards we walked back to The Elms for supper. A fresh breeze was blowing in from the sea and I noticed how animatedly my uncle was talking to Miss Hetherington as they walked in front.

'I thought perhaps Miss Fairclose would have wanted to see that play,' remarked Alistair.

'Well, she might have done. There is nothing to prevent her.'

'I meant to come with us.'

'Oh. Well, it's not likely that she would have suggested that. She knew the four of us were going together.'

'Yes. I was only thinking that she doesn't seem to have many friends yet.'

'That's hardly surprising. She hasn't lived in Southsands for very long. I expect she will have plenty of suitors soon and then she will be too busy to see very much of us.'

Alistair made no reply. I asked him if he thought my uncle was getting over my aunt's death now.

'Yes. He seems to have pulled himself together remarkably well lately. In fact,' he lowered his voice, 'Miss Hetherington's visits seem to be doing him a great deal of good.'

'I've noticed that, too.' I said.

'And do you mind?'

'Mind? No, there's no reason why I should. If they want to form a close friendship, I'm quite happy for them. I know Uncle Peter has always admired Miss Hetherington; he always approved of the way she ran her school. My aunt liked her as well — ' I broke off and Alistair squeezed my hand understandingly. We walked along in a companionable silence.

The seagulls were wheeling and screeching overhead and Southsands was preparing for the holiday season. I was walking along with a young man who cared for me, and would be only too happy to make me his wife. My uncle, whom I had been concerned about, seemed to be forming quite a close friendship with a lady whom I liked very much, and I had plenty of interests in my life now, and the companionship of Isabel Fairclose. Why, then, could I not be truly happy?

That night as Alistair was leaving the house to go back to his comfortable lodgings, he clasped me close to him. If I could not feel the same excitement which he appeared to when we embraced, did it matter so much?

Isabel was very interested in my relationship with Alistair.

'You are lucky,' she said. 'He's so nice. So charming and well-mannered, and such a clever doctor, too.'

I was rapidly making a new life for myself at Southsands. Old friends came back into my circle and I was asked to take Aunt Matilda's place in a number of charitable organisations. Meanwhile, Miss Hetherington and Uncle Peter seemed to be growing more and more attached to each other.

One evening Alistair and I were sitting in the drawing room. I had been playing the piano for him and he suddenly put his hand over mine.

'Marnie! Please listen to me. I've been very patient, but I feel I would like a more definite understanding between us now. If you still care for me, let us be engaged. I have spoken to your uncle about it and I have his blessing, but he says it is up to you.'

For a moment I sat without speaking, staring at the roses in the silver bowl on the piano. As I looked, a scarlet petal fell from a blossom. The room was filled with their fragrance on that warm, summer evening.

'I know you've had a difficult time since your return from Germany,' went on Alistair, 'but now I think you should put these unhappy things behind you — the shooting at that German castle and your aunt's death, although I know that is not so easily put to one side. But is seems to me you brood too much,

266

Marnie. Say that you will marry me.'

For a moment the room was silent, save for the ticking of the ormolu clock. The perfume of roses; Alistair's hand clasped over mine and the love in his eyes . . .

Doubts rose in me, even as his lips pressed against my hair.

'Say you'll marry me. I do love you, Marnie. I know that you care, too. I want to give you this ring, which belonged to my mother. Hold out your hand.'

Unprotestingly I allowed him to slip a solitaire diamond ring on the third finger of my left hand. 'If it doesn't fit, we can have it altered,' he said, and sealed the contract with a kiss.

This is all wrong, I told myself, and yet it was done. It might not be all wrong, anyway. It might be the right thing to do. My uncle was out, but as soon as he returned to the house we told him the news.

'I can't tell you how happy I am to hear this,' he said, shaking Alistair by the hand and kissing me. 'We shall have to celebrate the good news.'

'We won't be getting married just yet,' said Alistair. 'I think I surprised Marnie into this.'

I smiled, but there was more than a grain of truth in what he had said. And yet I felt a certain sense of relief. Things had been settled and I could put the past behind me. I was engaged to be married and I felt a glow of pride that such an eligible young man wanted me for his wife. I had a future now, a definite future to work towards.

Isabel and I continued to spend quite a lot of time in each other's company. On several occasions Alistair found himself escorting both of us, but he didn't seem to mind. I had thought that by now Isabel would have had a suitor of her own, as she was by no means indifferent to the opposite sex.

'There are not many really interesting young men at Southsands,' she would say if I brought the subject up.

'I think Mr. Alan Fletcher is quite interesting,' I said slyly. He was a member of our musical appreciation group. I had an idea that he liked Isabel — more than liked her, in fact. He was a solicitor, his father being the head of a prominent firm of solicitors in Southsands. I could not help thinking that he would be an ideal suitor for Isabel.

My uncle had announced his intention of giving me a ball to celebrate my engagement. I was on the point of protesting when I realised what great pleasure it would give him. So I agreed and said I was looking forward to it. Alistair was pleased, too, and said he thought it was time I met his father.

'It's going to be rather difficult just now,' he went on. 'Father is a doctor as you know, and I don't think it is very convenient to leave his practice just now. And I can't take you to Scotland to visit him and leave your uncle to cope. We'll work something out before too long, though.'

'Why did you come to Southsands when your own father had a practice?' I asked.

'I'm surprised you've never asked me that before! The reason is really quite simple. I didn't intend to start practising with my father and older brother. Father always encouraged Andrew to be a doctor, right from childhood. With me he was never so keen. However, he saw that I was determined and when I passed my first exams he said that if I 'managed' to qualify I would have to make my own arrangements as to where I practised. Andrew shares the practice in Edinburgh with him'

I was rather taken aback. I realised then how independent Alistair could be.

'Actually, Father is immensely proud of me now,' he continued with an amused twinkle in his eye. 'When I qualified he told me that he hadn't meant to sound condescending. He said I had never plodded on with my studies like Andrew and that a good, sharp prod was just what I needed! He might have been right about that, too. We're the best of friends, really. I've told him all about you, of course.'

There was pride in his voice when he said that, but I felt the faintest tremor of fear. It sounded so final. I was to be his wife; there was no doubt about that. Soon after that conversation I received a short but charming letter from his father, telling me how happy he was to hear of our engagement and how much he was looking forward to meeting me. The letter went on to say that he was attending a conference in London the following month and that he would like to spend a few days in Southsands if possible.

'Of course it's possible,' said my uncle as I read the last bit out over the breakfast table. 'He can stay here, naturally. And attend your engagement ball, I hope, Marnie.'

'Yes, that would be an agreeable idea if it is convenient for him,' I said, feeling a little nervous. Alistair's father had been a widower for many years, I knew. I had a mental picture of him as a somewhat dour and crusty Scot. Would I take to him? And he to me?

Alistair seemed pleased that I had received a letter and said he would be delighted if his father could stay and attend the ball.

I'm happy, I told myself. Everyone is pleased. I'm doing the right thing in marrying Alistair. My uncle is pleased; his father is pleased. It must be the right thing to do.

It must be — it must be! I repeated the words desperately to myself as I lay wakeful in bed. Then I made myself think about the new ball gown I was going to have. Because I would never again wear the cream-coloured one which I had worn to the ball at the schloss on the night of the murder.

My uncle and I had both discarded wearing mourning already, knowing how much my aunt had always hated it. Isabel and I had a trip to a London dressmaker to have new gowns made. Mrs. Fairclose accompanied us and I ordered a blue gown, while Isabel chose primrose yellow. We had an enjoyable, if somewhat exhausting day and travelled back on the train to Southsands, talking and laughing.

'Look, there's Miss Schwele!' exclaimed Isabel as we alighted from the carriage at Southsands. 'She must have been travelling from London on the same train. It looks as if you've lost your situation at Miss Hetherington's, Marnie. Although school will be breaking up in a couple of weeks, anyway.'

By this time Miss Schwele had seen us. She gave us a somewhat sad smile. I noticed that she was dressed in mourning. We greeted her and she told us that she had been back in England a couple of days and that she had been to London on business. Then, lapsing into German, she told us that her father had died and that, as she had a good position at Southsands, her mother was prepared to come to England, and that she wanted to buy a small but pleasant house in Southsands and then go back for her mother. She repeated this in English, for the benefit of Mrs. Fairclose, whom she knew from Isabel's schooldays.

As she was talking I saw Alistair slowly approaching us on the platform, obviously to give us time to finish our hurried conversation.

'You will not mind losing your teaching position next term, then?' Miss Schwele asked me.

'Not at all,' I said. 'I've only been keeping it open for you.'

'Many thanks, Marnie. By the way, Countess von Oldenburg has died. You know, the Dowager Countess. It was in the newspapers the same week as my poor father died. You must have known her.'

'Yes,' I said. 'I did. I'm sorry to hear of her death.' I knew that Miss Schwele's family lived near Goppertal.

'There is a gentleman to meet you; I must go. *Auf Wiedersehen*, Marnie, Isabel, Mrs. Fairclose.' She hurried away, nodding at us and including Alistair in her vague, sweet smile.

He greeted us all warmly, but remarked that I was looking a bit pale and that perhaps London had tired me.

274

'Perhaps,' I said.

'It's certainly tired me,' said Mrs. Fairclose with a smile.

'There is a hired carriage waiting,' said Alistair, and he helped us all into it, very solicitously. Mrs. Fairclose said we must all dine informally at her house. I knew that Uncle Peter was with Miss Hetherington for the evening, so I knew that I could not refuse her kind offer. I said little as the carriage bowled along.

'What is wrong, my dear?' came Mrs. Fairclose's voice. 'You seem to be very quiet, Marnie. Have you a headache? It was a bit trying in London.'

I felt myself flush, as all eyes were upon me. 'I was thinking about Miss Schwele and what she had told me,' I said hastily.

'She's the German mistress whose place Marnie has been taking,' Isabel explained to Alistair. 'She's going to buy a house here and bring her mother over to live now that her father has died. Eventually I should think they will become naturalised British citizens. Oh, but that probably wasn't what Marnie meant; she mentioned about a Countess dying at that schloss where Marnie was a governess.'

'I don't think Marnie likes to be reminded of that shooting tragedy,' said Alistair hastily, trying to be helpful.

'What shooting tragedy?' asked Isabel, agog with curiosity. I had never mentioned it to her.

'The Countess was shot dead while Marnie was there,' explained Alistair briefly. I could tell that Mrs. Fairclose was as fascinated as her daughter, but she had to set a good example.

'But Miss Schwele said the Countess had died recently,' exclaimed Isabel.

'She means the Dowager Countess. She had been ill for some time,' I said.

'I should think you're glad you left when you did. It doesn't sound a very cheerful place. You must tell me all about the shooting,' said Isabel rather tactlessly.

'Isabel! You mustn't talk about things

276

like that lightly,' said her mother sharply. 'You sound quite frivolous. Marnie lost her aunt last winter and poor Miss Schwele herself is in mourning for her father. Death is not a joke, as Dr. Harlow can tell you.'

Isabel looked suitably chastened, but Alistair remarked kindly that he was sure she hadn't meant to be frivolous. I was relieved when the carriage entered the drive of the charming Regency house which the Faircloses had bought for their retirement.

The remainder of the evening was an ordeal. The news imparted by Miss Schwele had a profound effect on me. I remembered the Dowager Countess; her dignified presence and her cultured mind. How bravely she had borne her illness, and what a dreadful shock it must have been for her to learn of Maria's death. In my mind's eye I could see her funeral procession wending its way down the mountain road to the church of St. Nicholaus. People would be gathered there to pay their last respects to Countess Adelaide von Oldenburg. Then the cortege would return and she would be laid to rest in the burial ground with her husband. I pictured poor Charlotte weeping at the graveside, with the Count's arm around her. There would be summer flowers on the grave . . .

'Marnie, you really do look tired.' There was a note of concern in Alistair's voice. 'I think I ought to take you home now. Do excuse us both, Mrs. Fairclose. It's been a delightful evening.'

I did not protest. When I was finally in my room some time later, I sat down in front of the dressing table and removed my engagement ring before brushing my hair. Slowly I made my toilet and crept into bed. Even as I did so I knew that there would be no chance of sleep.

I relived that night in the schloss; that unforgettable night. The sound of sobbing; *Fraulein* Krupp at my door; the scene in Countess Maria's room as she lay there dead.

And the Count, seemingly stunned by what had happened; the Count whom I had loved so deeply, in whose arms I had once been clasped . . . just once . . .

I turned over in bed again. I was engaged to marry Alistair Harlow and I had been to London that very day to buy a new ball gown for our engagement ball. I began to weep. I should not have accepted Alistair's proposal of marriage. I saw that now, with terrible clarity. What I felt for him was not love; would never be love. Perhaps if I tried, though, I could be happy with him, knowing how much he cared for me and how much he wanted me for his wife. Anyway, it was too late for me to change my mind now. And if I married Alistair I would be marrying a dedicated man, a man whom I could respect for the work he did.

It was growing light before I fell asleep.

11

'I've brought back a few German newspapers,' said Miss Schwele. 'I thought the girls might like to look at them and no doubt you will too. Here's the one with the obituary in about the Countess' death.'

'Thank you very much,' I said, taking it from her. I glanced round the classroom. School broke up the following week and Miss Schwele had called in to see the headmistress and to let the girls know that she would be back for the Autumn term.

As soon as I was alone I turned the pages of the newspaper until I came to the piece about the Countess. It mentioned all the charities she had been active in and the tireless work which she had done during the Franco-Prussian war. The obituary went on to say that the chief mourners were her son, Count Carl von Oldenburg and her granddaughter, Charlotte. To my surprise the funeral service was held in The Sacred Heart, the Catholic Church in Goppertal. The obituary also mentioned the tragedy at Schloss Beissel the year before, when Countess Maria had been shot. The case was, apparently, still open. The shooting remained a mystery. I folded up the newspaper and stared unseeingly in front of me for a few minutes.

Then I resolutely turned my thoughts to the present. There was plenty to think about, not least of which was the forthcoming visit of Alistair's father and the engagement ball. Dr. Harlow senior turned out to be a slim, rather humorous Scot; a keen golf-player and a dedicated medical man. He and my uncle got on very well indeed, and he appeared to regard me as a highly suitable wife for his son. Naturally, there was a certain amount of talk about medical matters.

'I've left an outbreak of diphtheria

behind me,' remarked Dr. Harlow as we were finishing dinner on the evening of his arrival. 'Have you got it at Southsands?'

'We've had a couple of cases. Nothing like an epidemic yet, though,' Uncle Peter replied. 'We don't want it, either.'

'Indeed, you don't! There are always a few cases around, of course. That was an excellent dinner, my dear — ' he turned to me, his eyes kindly behind his spectacles. 'You do the honours very prettily.'

I smiled at him. It was plain that he thought I was an admirable hostess, a wife who would be a credit to his son. Alistair and my uncle both looked gratified; I felt myself to be the centre of attention. If only the three men present at that table could have known the truth! That although I was betrothed to Alistair Harlow, my thoughts were with another man; a man who had not denied that he had been responsible for his wife's death . . .

'As soon as it is convenient, you and

Alistair must come and stay with me,' continued Dr. Harlow senior. 'When you can spare him, of course,' he added jovially to my uncle. He then went on to say that he had heard I had been teaching German temporarily.

'Yes. The German mistress at my old school here had to go back to Germany when her father was taken ill, so the headmistress asked me if I would take her place for the time being. The school has broken up now for the summer holidays, but the German mistress will be back next term in any case.'

'So you are a lady of leisure again,' commented Alistair's father.

'Well, not quite,' put in my uncle. 'Marnie runs the household.'

'Yes, of course. And very well, too,' said Dr. Harlow hastily.

'You must meet Marnie's former headmistress. She is a close friend of mine, a charming person,' said Uncle Peter.

The evening passed pleasantly. Much later, undressing in my room, I wished that my uncle had not been so insistent on giving me an engagement ball. He seemed to think that it was the right gesture on his part, saying that I deserved it. It made things seem so irrevocably settled. The thought came to me that it was not too late to break things off between myself and Alistair. Or instead, could I say to him, 'I don't think that I really love you, although I like you very much. I love another man, but he has gone out of my life for ever. Do you think that if we get married, we will be happy?'

It was all so complicated; so hopeless.

★ ★ ★

'Are you sure you are feeling alright, Dr. Harlow?' I enquired of Alistair's father as he stood sipping brandy and, I thought, looking far from well.

'My dear, it's nothing. Just a slight indisposition. It will have passed off by tomorrow. It will have to, I assure you, as they need me back home as soon as possible. Now, I believe this is my dance?'

It was the evening of my engagement ball. Uncle Peter had hired an impressive hall and an orchestra of some repute. The floral decorations were charming and it was plain that my uncle had spared no expense. There were quite a number of guests, more than I had anticipated when the idea had first been mooted. I had written all the invitations myself, which had made me realise just how well-known my uncle was in Southsands, as he had wanted all his friends to be there as well as mine. Not surprisingly, the guests were of all ages, from school chums of mine to some of my uncle's older patients. His life-long friend, Dr. Hargreaves, was there; the doctor who had attended me from childhood.

A big disappointment for Uncle Peter was that Miss Hetherington was unable to be at the ball. She had been called suddenly to the bedside of an elderly aunt who was very ill. We had invited

Aunt Matilda's sister, Alice, but she had declined, saying she had a touch of rheumatism, but that she was pleased to hear of my engagement to Alistair 'as dear Matilda always hoped for it.'

As I waltzed with Dr. Harlow I caught sight of Alistair dancing with Isabel. She was wearing the very becoming gown which had been made for her in London; primrose yellow suited her to perfection. I was startled by the expression on her face, though. It was a strangely brooding, inward look. She seemed oblivious of everyone.

I had no time to think about such matters, though. I was too busy smiling at people and thanking them for their kind wishes. All eyes were upon me and I found it quite a strain. I had taken to Alistair's father and he seemed to have taken to me, too. For the past two days, though, he had not looked well. I felt rather concerned, as the following day he was travelling back to Edinburgh. He had, however, assured me twice that he was alright and, as he pointed out, he was a doctor.

Alistair and I were toasted in champagne and the supper was delicious, with every sweet and savoury imaginable. Uncle Peter made a brief speech saying how much my engagement had pleased him, and he was well clapped, being a very popular man. So was Alistair, who was congratulated throughout the evening.

I was paid many compliments and my new blue gown was much admired. I tried to keep my mind in the present, but it was inevitable that I should be reminded of that last ball I had attended at the schloss. It seemed an age ago although, in fact, it was less than a year. How strange that, just as I was attempting to settle down in Southsands and accept the idea of becoming Alistair's wife, an obituary in a foreign newspaper could bring back all the heartache. What a terrible place the schloss must be now.

Alistair claimed a dance. 'I'm sure your father is not well,' I said, as we moved onto the floor.

'Don't fuss over him, dear. He never will admit to not feeling well. He often gets colds which he denies having. He's best left alone.'

I dropped the subject and we danced in silence. Somehow I sensed that Alistair was not enjoying himself as much as he had appeared to earlier in the evening. To my surprise, as soon as my dance with him was over, Mrs. Fairclose approached me and told me that they were taking Isabel home, as she did not feel well.

'Isabel not well?' I exclaimed. 'She seemed quite well earlier in the evening — '

'A headache,' her mother explained. Mrs. Fairclose was wearing a striking magenta ball gown which became her well. She seemed oddly flustered, though, wafting her fan with a slightly agitated movement. 'She's had a wonderful time, anyway and the ball will be drawing to a close before long.'

'I'll say goodnight to her — ' I caught

sight of Isabel going in the direction of the ladies' cloakroom.

'She asked me to make her apologies. She wants to slip away as unobtrusively as possible,' said her mother quickly. Evidently for some reason she preferred me not to speak to Isabel just then. 'It would make her feel better if you carried on dancing, as if she had not left early. Goodnight, Marnie, it's been a most enjoyable evening; do thank your uncle on behalf of our family.'

Naturally, there was nothing I could do except what she had requested, although I felt rather puzzled. Alistair had left my side for a few minutes, but when he returned I told him that Isabel had gone home.

'She has a headache, apparently,' I said.

'Has she, indeed? I hope it's nothing much,' was his comment. After that he seemed very quiet. I was relieved when the ball was over at last. I had not enjoyed it very much. Alistair's father was obviously unwell, despite his protests to the contrary, and Isabel had left early, indisposed.

Alistair was silent and subdued; one would not have thought that he had just been to his engagement ball. Nobody said much when we were finally bowling home through the deserted streets of Southsands.

My uncle looked well satisfied, though, in spite of the fact that he had been disappointed by Miss Hetherington's absence. I felt my love for him rise as he smiled at me. He was so kind, and he thought he had done his duty by me, giving me such a splendid engagement ball.

'Well, I expect we are all a bit tired,' he remarked as we entered the quiet house. Alistair had been staying with us during the time of his father's visit, so he did not have to go back to his usual lodgings.

'I shall have to be up at a reasonably early hour tomorrow,' his father said. 'It's been a delightful evening. I wouldn't have missed it for anything.

The next event will be the wedding.'

'As soon as Marnie names the day . . . ' my uncle broke off, smiling at me.

I made no reply, merely smiled back automatically.

'Are you alright, Father?' enquired Alistair.

'Yes. A little tired, perhaps. I'll retire immediately, if you will all excuse me.'

'Would you care for a nightcap? Brandy? Whisky?' enquired Uncle Peter. I reflected that they were all three doctors, so there was no point in my fussing over Alistair's father. I kissed them all goodnight and left them in the drawing room. My emotions were too confused to be sorted out at that late hour. I wanted to get to bed as soon as possible. I could manage my toilet without a maid to help me, thanks to my training at the *Damenstift*. Alone in my room, I undressed and climbed into bed, feeling unbelievably weary.

It had been a lovely summer day, but it was high tide now and a fresh breeze had blown in from the sea. My window was open and I was grateful for the gust of cool air on my face. I closed my eyes and sleep came surprisingly quickly. It was not a restful slumber, though. I had a series of vivid, unpleasant dreams; a kind of kaleidoscope of nightmares. I dreamt that I was dancing, but not with Alistair. I was in the arms of Carl von Oldenburg, then suddenly he was torn away from me. I followed him through the endless corridors of the schloss. He was surrounded by policemen. At last they pushed open a door and there inside I beheld the murdered body of Maria.

'Did you do it? Did you do it?' I heard myself screaming. Then I became aware of someone shaking me gently. It was Tina.

'Miss Marnie! Miss Marnie! You're dreaming — you've overslept!' There was concern on her plump, rosy face. I struggled to sit up. I was wet with perspiration. For a few moments I felt bewildered. This was not the schloss; I was safe at home.

'Oh . . . yes. I've been dreaming,' I mumbled. 'What time is it?'

'It's nine o'clock and Dr. Harlow — not young Dr. Harlow, his father — will shortly be leaving the house. He don't seem so well to me. Mrs. McNulty said he never ate a bit of breakfast, but there you are. I'm sorry I woke you so suddenly.'

'I'm glad you did.' I said, beginning to collect my wits. 'Have you brought my hot water?'

'I brought it some time ago. I've been up before, you know. It's not very hot now — do you want fresh?'

'No, don't bother. I'll be down directly,' I said, getting out of bed. Tina left the room. As I washed in the near-cold water it was hard to shake off the strong impression that the dream had left, that I was back in the schloss. So Tina did not think that Alistair's father was very well. No doubt she was right, but, well or ill, he was leaving for London today to take the northbound train to Edinburgh. I hurried through my toilet and hastened down to the breakfast room. My uncle was there alone.

'Good morning, Marnie. I sent Tina up to you. I would not have done under normal circumstances, but, as you know, Alistair's father is going back today. Are you alright?'

'Of course. I just overslept. Is Dr. Harlow feeling any better today?'

Uncle Peter gave a non-committal shrug. 'He says he's well enough to travel — says it's nothing. He and Alistair are upstairs at the moment, attending to last minute tasks. I shall have to be on my rounds shortly. Alistair is seeing his father off, naturally. If you hurry, perhaps you can join him.'

'Yes, I will. I only want a cup of coffee for breakfast,' I said. It was true, I had no appetite for food. That awful dream and the feeling of being back in Schloss Beissel . . . and how was Isabel today? I would have to find out.

Just over half an hour later I said

goodbye to Dr. Harlow at Southsands station. I thought how white and drawn he looked. Alistair seemed very serious and abstracted. They shook hands and once again I kissed his father. As soon as we had waved the train out Alistair remarked that his father had admitted to feeling very tired.

'He should be able to sleep on the journey,' I said.

Alistair still looked worried, though. He put his hand under my elbow as we ascended the steps and came out of the station into the bright sunlight of the day. Southsands was full of summer visitors; families drove by in open carriages or walked along sedately, taking the air. Outside the station an organ-grinder with a monkey began to play a tinkling tune. A depression, like a black cloud, settled over me. I could see no happiness ahead for me; none if I married Alistair and none if I didn't. I felt suddenly completely isolated from the busy, bustling crowd and, to my dismay, I found that I was beginning to cry. It was ridiculous, in full view of everyone, on a bright, sunny day.

'What is wrong, Marnie? Oh, dear, let's get into the carriage.'

He helped me into the waiting vehicle and I sat and sobbed with his arm around me. For a couple who had recently attended a ball to celebrate our engagement, we did not make a very joyful pair.

In silence we drove back to The Elms. By the time we descended from the carriage I had more control over myself. I knew that my eyes would be red, but I was outwardly composed as I entered the house. I sat down in the morning room and removed my hat.

'I'm afraid I shall have to visit some patients now,' said Alistair. 'I don't like to leave you under the circumstances, dear. I don't know what's upset you, but I think you should have a rest this morning. It was late when you got to bed last night. You would probably have slept much longer if Tina hadn't woken you up this morning.'

'I was glad to be woken up, as a matter of fact. I was having nightmares. I think I'll rest today. Perhaps you'll call and see how Isabel is.'

'Yes, I will certainly do that. What with you and Father and Isabel not very well . . . ' he broke off and shook his head. Then he gave me a quick kiss and, with a wave, he was gone.

I rose and went slowly upstairs. I would lie down for a while, until luncheon, anyway. Although I officially ran the house, Mrs. McNulty needed few instructions from me. I usually suggested the menu for dinner, but little beside that. I opened my bedroom door and closed it behind me noiselessly. Tina and Mrs. McNulty would fuss over me if they thought I was not well, and I didn't want them fussing. I just wanted to be alone, to try and collect my thoughts.

I opened my dressing table drawer and took out the obituary which I had cut from the German newspaper. Again I read it and again I wondered why the

Dowager Countess' funeral service had been held at the Catholic church. I would never know. In any case, she was buried; the brave, proud, elegant Countess Adelaide von Oldenburg. Now there was no female von Oldenburg at the schloss, apart from the youthful Charlotte. I wondered if the Count had sent her to the *Damenstift*, as I had suggested. Or was she shut up there by herself, moping, with the dreadful Gertrud Krupp hounding her footsteps? But no, I would not think of it.

I lay on the bed and tried to make my mind a blank. Why had I been so forcibly reminded of Schloss Beissel just as I was settling down to the idea of marrying Alistair? I closed my eyes and wondered what was wrong with Isabel. I wondered, too, if Alistair's father was feeling any better. Later in the day I would see Alistair again and he would try to find out why I had been so upset. I myself could not understand why the tears had suddenly come to my eyes.

Rather to my surprise I fell asleep again and woke with a start, bewildered, to find myself lying on the bed fully dressed. The next moment there was a tap at the door.

'Come in,' I called. It was Uncle Peter.

'How are you, my dear?' he asked, his voice very gentle. 'Alistair tells me you weren't feeling very well after seeing Dr. Harlow off.'

'It's nothing,' I assured him, sitting up. 'I had a bad night last night and evidently I didn't have enough sleep. I've just woken up again. Goodness, is that the time?'

'Yes. Luncheon is ready. Alistair said he would call round this evening. I asked him to have luncheon with us today, but he declined. It's been a bit topsy-turvy here lately, with both Alistair and his father staying. I think he wants to reassure Mrs. Briggs that she hasn't lost him altogether as a lodger. I'll see you in the dining room presently, then.'

He closed the door. I rose from the bed and tidied myself up. My face was paler than usual. I pinched some colour into it and went downstairs. I had little appetite, but made some pretence of eating, as I did not wish to draw further comment from my uncle.

'I must say I enjoyed Dr. Harlow's companionship,' he remarked. 'He's pretty hard-pressed in his practice with his other son, now that they have this outbreak of diphtheria. When these epidemics start — ' he shook his head.

Tina brought in the second postal delivery of the day. Uncle Peter's face brightened as he opened a cream-coloured envelope. 'It's from Miss Hetherington,' he exclaimed. 'She's coming back in a couple of days. It seems that her aunt is rallying, despite her great age. She is very sorry she was unable to attend your engagement ball.'

'We're just as sorry,' I said rather absently.

'I expect you miss teaching the girls.' My uncle spoke sympathetically. He put the letter away. 'I can tell you're a bit upset. Personally, I think you could do with a holiday. There is such a thing as delayed shock. You've coped with some big strains over the past twelve months. It's surprising how people can keep going through one crisis after another and then they seem to have a reaction. If you feel energetic enough, a walk down to the sea front would do you a lot of good. I wish that I could accompany you, but I'm tied up this afternoon with patients. Lie down for a while again after luncheon and then have a walk out. It's a lovely day. It would be better, naturally, if you had the companionship of Isabel. Alistair said he would be calling to see how she is today.'

'Yes, I think I will have a walk,' I said, pushing my pudding to one side.

Accordingly, about an hour later, I walked slowly down to the sea front. It was warm, but there was a slight breeze stirring the cornfields around Southsands. I knew the way to the promenade so well that I walked along without any conscious sense of direction. I walked past shops selling jewellery, tobacco and drapery, past churches and chapels and across roads crowded with carriages and high-stepping horses. At last I reached the great frontage of hotels with flowered balconies, facing directly onto the sea. I sat down on a green-painted seat. Ahead of me was the ocean, dazzling in the afternoon sun, with the pier stretching out like a pointing finger. A young man and a girl walked by, arm in arm, obviously in love. The strangely cut-off feeling which I had experienced that morning came back to me. I felt miles away from these happy holiday-makers. The sound of people talking and laughing and the glad play-cries of children seemed to belong to another world. As I sat there it came to me more and more strongly that I was not in love with Alistair, and that it would be wrong of me to marry him. It was not just that I would be untrue to myself if I did so; it would not be fair to Alistair either. He had mentioned on more than one occasion that he was making allowances for the fact that I'd had so many unhappy experiences over the past twelve months, but was he uneasy about things in his heart?

Of course, I was fond of him and had a great respect for his dedication to medicine, but was that enough for a truly happy union? I should never have allowed myself to become engaged to him. And yet, was I only thinking like this because I'd had news, albeit indirect, of Schloss Beissel? It had evoked Carl von Oldenburg's presence vividly; too vividly for my peace of mind. I thought of Aunt Matilda and her simple belief in omens, about which my uncle had often teased her. Before embarking on anything new, even some fund-raising for charity, she would talk about 'good omens'. Was getting news of the schloss just before my engagement ball an omen?

I sat and wrestled with my emotions, feeling pulled first one way and then another, but getting no nearer a solution. One thing was certain, though.

Engaged we may be, but I would see that there was no speedy wedding . . .

I was sitting alone in the drawing room that evening when Alistair called. He greeted me with a gentle kiss and asked me how I was feeling.

'Much better, thank you,' I replied, and in a way it was true. I felt that the best thing to do was to wait a few months and then see how things were between myself and Alistair.

'I'm pleased to hear it. I called in to see Isabel this afternoon,' he went on.

'Yes? And is she well again?'

He did not reply immediately. Instead he walked over to the window and stood looking at the garden, rich with the colours and scents of high summer. 'She has an aunt at Cromer,' he said slowly. 'Her mother is of the opinion that she should go and stay with her for the rest of the summer.'

'From what Isabel has told me, she does not greatly care for visits to that aunt.'

'Perhaps not, but it might be a good idea.'

I was puzzled and, moreover, vaguely resentful that Isabel should be considering leaving Southsands for a while. It was the suddenness of it all that baffled me. She had not even wished to speak to me the night before when she had left the ball so abruptly.

'The strange behaviour of some people . . . ' I murmured.

'Yes, people do behave strangely, dear. You did yourself this morning.'

He was right, of course. My uncle joined us in the drawing room and the three of us played solo whist for the remainder of the evening. It was not a satisfactory day at all, and the following morning I woke up firmly resolved to visit Isabel and to find out what was going on.

It was another hot, sunny day and I decided to walk there. In a cream silk dress with matching hat and parasol, I set out shortly after luncheon. The shops looked very gay with their striped awnings to keep their wares from being faded. A horse in a straw bonnet was drawing the watering cart to keep the dust on the roads down and the smell of the water on the dust was as pleasurable to me as it had been as a child. The traffic on the roads was as heavy and varied as it had been the day before; the butchers' carts drawn by swiftly-trotting horses, brewers' drays by shire horses with polished brasses and victorias carrying elegant ladies.

It was quite a long walk to where Isabel lived and I was glad when I reached Prince's Square, with its fine Regency houses. I walked up the drive of Hove House. A gardener was busy hoeing the flowerbeds. He raised his cap as I went past him and I smiled. I rang the doorbell; the pretty dark-eyed maid answered it and showed me into the drawing room. It was very stylish, newly-decorated in white and gold.

After about ten minutes had elapsed, Isabel's mother appeared in the room, looking rather embarrassed.

'Good day, Marnie. How are you? Er . . . I'm afraid Isabel will not be able to see you.'

I felt completely taken aback. 'She is not well, then?' I enquired dubiously.

'I'm afraid not.' Mrs. Fairclose's eyes seemed to be avoiding mine. 'She is not at home to anyone. I'm sorry.'

'Not at home?'

Mrs. Fairclose shook her head, looking extremely ill-at-ease. It was plain that I was not welcome there. I stood up, deciding to spare her any further embarrassment.

'I'm sorry to hear that,' I said in a composed tone of voice. 'Never mind, another time, perhaps.'

I thought of the many occasions on which Isabel had called informally at our house and taken afternoon tea with us. Her mother did not offer me tea; instead she appeared highly relieved that I was going, and rang for the maid to see me out. I took a deep breath of the warm air outside as I retraced my footsteps. I wouldn't go to that house again in a hurry, I thought. At the same time, I felt bewildered and hurt by Isabel's peculiar behaviour.

There was a delightful park facing onto Prince's Square. There were seats and flowerbeds and a tiny lake where small boys sailed toy boats. I rolled up my parasol and sat down under a tree. There was no reason why I should rush back home. Besides, I wanted to try to understand Isabel's refusal to see me. Had I offended her without knowing it?

As I sat there I saw a trap drive into the square and through the gates of Hove House. There was something familiar about that trap — yes, of course! It was our trap. When my uncle was using it Alistair visited the patients on horseback, but I knew that he had the use of the trap that afternoon. So he was visiting Isabel again.

No doubt Mrs. Fairclose would tell him that he had just missed me. Well, he wouldn't be there for more than fifteen minutes at the most. I would wait for him at the end of Prince's Square and he could drive me home. Accordingly, after about ten minutes, I unfurled my parasol again and rose, walking slowly across the sun-baked grass. I retraced my footsteps to the pavement where Prince's Square began and sauntered up and down. Fifteen minutes passed and there was no sign of Alistair.

I went back and sat in the park again. Half an hour later I was still sitting there. Alistair had been in the house three-quarters of an hour and I had been told that Isabel was not at home to anyone. She was at home to him, evidently, and no professional visit should take that long, except for a confinement. What was going on? I would find out that evening. Alistair had said that he would be round to see me. I waited a few minutes longer and then rose and walked back to the house, feeling dispirited and ill-at-ease.

It was quite late that evening when Alistair arrived. My uncle was taking his evening surgery and I was alone in the drawing room. I decided to wait and let him mention his visit to Hove House first, but this he did not do.

Piqued, I said nothing about mine, either. Nor did I tell my uncle where I had been that afternoon. Isabel's behaviour was so strange and so hurtful, and Alistair's conduct so deceitful that I could not have revealed my hurt feelings to anyone. Both Alistair and I were very quiet that evening and it was a relief to me when my uncle joined us.

Just when Alistair was on the point of going, Tina tapped on the drawing room door and said that Mrs. Briggs' maid had come to the house with a telegram for Dr. Harlow.

'Bring her in here, then,' said Uncle Peter, looking rather nervous.

'If you please, Sir, it's a telegram, and Mrs. Briggs said it might be urgent. She said you would most likely be here,' said the maid, dropping a curtsey and appearing somewhat flustered at being brought into our drawing room.

'Thank you, Ellen,' said Alistair, taking it from her. He opened it and read it, his brows drawing together.

'Not bad news, I hope,' said my uncle.

'Yes, I'm afraid it is. It's from my brother. My father is very ill; it's diphtheria.'

'What will you do? Go up there straight away?' enquired Uncle Peter.

'I'll wire back and ask if it's necessary for me to go just now. If Andrew will keep me informed — ' he broke off, looking extremely worried. 'When did it arrive?' he asked the maid.

'About an hour ago, Sir'

'It's too late to wire now. I'll wire in the morning,' said Alistair.

'I'll drive you and the girl back in the trap,' offered Uncle Peter.

I felt shocked by the news and sorry for Alistair, but just then there was little or nothing that I could do.

The following morning Alistair received another telegram. It was to say that his father had died. I could scarcely believe it.

'He must have felt ill for several days before he finally took to his bed,' remarked my uncle. 'He must have been running a temperature while he was here . . . I've never heard of anyone his age going down with diphtheria. Young adults, yes. Your parents — ' he broke off, looking at me with sudden concern. 'You kissed him goodnight after the ball, didn't you?'

'Yes, and at the station.'

'Well, you'd better gargle twice a day, just as a precaution.'

Alistair, white-faced, prepared to go immediately to Edinburgh. I suggested that I should travel there with him, but he would not hear of it.

'You've had enough problems of your own, Marnie, without coming to a house of bereavement. No, stay here with your uncle. I'll write to you.'

My uncle was sympathetic towards Alistair and said that he could manage by himself for a couple of weeks, or longer if need be. We saw Alistair off at Southsands station, and it was hard for me to believe that such a short while ago I had waved his father off on the same journey.

Back in the house I developed a throbbing headache, which persisted for the rest of the day. It grew so bad that I was unable to dine with my uncle and retired to bed early, after gargling dutifully with the prescribed disinfectant. The following day my headache eased off, but I had a feeling of extreme lassitude.

'It's the shock,' pronounced my uncle. 'Dr. Harlow was such a splendid fellow; he was so pleased about you and Alistair, too. He told me that if he could have chosen a wife for his son, he would have chosen you.'

I smiled, with an effort. It was gratifying to be regarded so highly, and I was pleased that Dr. Harlow had enjoyed his stay with us, but now I myself felt unwell. Each night I would go to bed, hoping that I would feel better on the morrow, but the malaise persisted. I had a short but affectionate letter from Alistair, telling me about the funeral and various other details. I wrote back, but refrained from saying that I did not feel well.

I rested every day, spending a good deal of time lying on my bed, and if Tina and Mrs. McNulty fussed I told them I was trying to get over the shock of Dr. Harlow's sudden death. I wondered if Isabel Fairclose had heard about it. Well, she had not heard about it from me, at all events. I had told my uncle that I understood she was going on a visit to Cromer, when he remarked that she had not been to the house lately. He did not pursue the subject, probably, I thought, because he was extremely busy trying to cope with all his patients without Alistair's assistance.

I was still assiduously gargling, but one evening I had to admit to myself that my throat felt peculiar, and that it hurt to swallow. I examined it in the mirror. It was inflamed, and my tonsils and the back of my throat appeared to be covered with a curious grey membrane. I knew that Uncle Peter was attending a confinement; I had dined alone, although in fact I had eaten scarcely anything. I went to bed, drawing the curtains to shut out the brightness of the summer evening.

That night I tossed and turned in a fever, and when morning came I knew that I was too ill to attempt to rise. When Tina brought in my hot water I told her so in a hoarse whisper.

'Oh, Miss Marnie!' she exclaimed, setting down the ewer. 'I'll tell the doctor — ' she hurried away. I tried to swallow, but found it almost impossible. The perspiration was running off me in rivulets. Somehow, nothing seemed very important. I ached all over and felt terribly weak. The next thing I knew, Uncle Peter was at my beside.

'Marnie!' With an effort I opened my heavy eyes and saw the fear on his face. I was aware that he was taking my pulse and my temperature.

'Open your mouth — let me look — ' he was holding my tongue down with something and peering at my throat. He suddenly stood away from the bed and

I closed my eyes again. I felt terribly ill; never in my life had I felt like this.

'I want a drink,' I managed to whisper, 'but I can't swallow.'

After that my life was like a waking dream; a period when night merged into day; when there was someone constantly at my bedside and someone always seemed to be doing things to me. I remember lying there with no thought in my mind except how I was going to breathe. Indeed, it seemed to me that I was dying; that this was the end. Or was I dreaming?

I relived the whole cavalcade of my life from early childhood. I was a little girl again, rambling on the Downs with my uncle. I could feel the short, dry grass beneath my feet and smell the tansy, thyme and chamomile; above was the enormous arc of the sky where larks soared all day. Then I was on the seashore, licking the salt tang from my lips as I collected shells. I was watching the dancing bear; the Punch and Judy show; the pierrots. I was sitting before a glowing fire, listening to the sound of the muffin man's bell.

I was a schoolgirl at Miss Hetherington's school again, eagerly taking part in all the activities. I was back in Germany, with *Frau* Krafft welcoming me to the *Damenstift*. It was Christmas and I stood beneath a decorated fir tree singing '*Stille Nacht, Heilig Nacht*'. Holding Isabel's hand I was skating, with a keen wind stinging my face . . .

The scene changed. I was at Schloss Beissel, talking to Charlotte. I could smell the mustiness of the schloss and see the liveried footmen in powdered wigs and white gloves. The gloomy grandeur of that castle enveloped me once more. Faces stared at me from all sides; the proud, lined face of Countess Adelaide; the plain features of Gertrud Krupp. There was a man's face as finely chiselled as a coin, with a scar on the cheekbone. I saw the lovely countenance of his wife, Maria, mocking me like a tiny elegant ghost. I was in a hunting lodge then, with the sound of

German *Lieder* being played on a fiddle, filling my very soul with unbearable sadness . . . I saw Countess Maria lying on her bed, blood-stained and dead.

A young girl was sobbing. In a broken voice she whispered, '*Auf wiedersehen.*' She could not bear the idea that she would never see me again. Then I heard the sound of church bells. I was standing on the mountainside and Carl von Oldenburg was there, too, but several yards away. The bells began to echo and I tried to go to him, but seemed rooted to the spot.

'Come to me!' I whispered. 'Come to me — my dearest Count!' He never moved, and I spoke in German: '*Ich liebe dich! Ich liebe dich!*'

Then a hand clasped mine and voice murmured, 'Marnie.'

'Carl.' I struggled to sit up. '*Liebling, liebling* — ' the words of love died away as my very throat seemed to seize up. It was terrifying; I was choking to death.

12

I was aware of pale sunlight filtering onto the rose-patterned wallpaper in my room. I lay and looked at the bright patch which faded and came back again. I was too weak to move and, indeed, I had no desire to do so.

I could swallow again; the dreadful choking, suffocating sensation had gone and just then that was all that mattered. Gradually, the familiar things in my room began to take shape. I could see my bookcase, still with some of my childhood books in, and my wardrobe and dressing-table. The sampler which I had embroidered as an eight-year-old was hanging on the wall with the old, well-loved pictures. My gaze travelled over the trinket box which I had made out of shells collected from the seashore; over the wax doll, Emmeline, which my aunt and uncle had bought for me when I had first come to live with them. Then I looked at the white cloth on my bedside table and the clutter of bottles on it, showing that it was a sick-room. I felt a faint interest in the outside world. For some time I gazed around and then the door was opened and my uncle entered the room.

'Marnie! You are awake — and feeling much better, thank goodness.' He hurried to my bedside.

'Yes,' I whispered weakly, trying to smile. 'How long have I been ill?'

'You've been very ill indeed for the past ten days . . . it's been terrible . . . ' He shook his head, unable to convey his anguish at my illness, or his relief that I was recovering. He sat down on the bed and blew his nose. I could see that his emotion was beyond words. Tears of weakness filled my eyes and rolled unheeded down my cheeks.

'There, don't upset yourself, dear. I'll get Tina to bring you up something to eat — just a tasty morsel, to tempt your appetite. I expect you are very thirsty, too. It will take a long time to build you up again.'

Memories came rushing back to me. Alistair had lost his father and had gone to Edinburgh.

'Has Alistair come back yet?' I asked.

'Yes. He's spent quite a lot of time at your bedside. We've taken it in turns to sit with you. Dr. Hargreaves has been looking after you officially.'

Yes, of course, he would, I thought. Dear old Dr. Hargreaves.

'I've had three doctors to care for me, then,' I said slowly.

'You have, all told. Dr. Hargreaves officially, myself and Alistair unofficially.'

I noticed how worn and tired my uncle looked. 'I've been a terrible nuisance.' I said. 'What has been wrong with me?' I knew, though, before he uttered the dreaded word.

'Diphtheria. You must have caught it from Alistair's father. It's not a summer disease, really; it's an autumn and winter thing, although it can linger through to spring.'

'I thought I had just caught a chill or something. I didn't want to make a fuss. I felt afraid when I looked at my throat in the mirror the night before Tina brought you to me. You were out that night, though. Even then, I couldn't really believe the worst — it developed so quickly.'

'Diphtheria has a very short incubation period.'

'It seems to haunt our family, doesn't it?'

'It haunts a number of families, I'm afraid. We have a few cases on our hands in Southsands.'

'Is Miss Hetherington home again?'

'She is, and I'm thankful for that. You've no idea how wonderful she has been, Marnie. I forbade her to come to the house because of the risk of infection, but she has written a letter every day. Tina and Mrs. McNulty both had it as children, fortunately, so they have no fear of infection. Alistair and I seem to bear charmed lives — well, up to now. Pray some day they will find a vaccine against it, like with small-pox. Anyway, even now that the acute phase is over, you will have to stay in bed for at least one month, Marnie, as the diphtheria toxin is particularly poisonous to the heart. But don't worry about that; you are going to get perfectly well again. We are just going to take every care that you do.'

The rest of the day passed quickly, in a kind of blur, as it always seems to do after the worst of an illness is over. Alistair came to see me in the evening. He, too, looked pale and drawn.

'Good evening, Marnie. I hear you are much better.' He approached the bed and stood looking down at me. There was a very subdued air about him and I thought straight away of his father.

'You've had a dreadful time,' I murmured. 'Your poor father . . . and I — ' I broke off.

'It was a terrible shock about my

father,' he said. 'And no sooner was the funeral over than I heard from your uncle that you had fallen a victim. My brother told me that he would sort out all Father's affairs, and I took the train back here at the earliest possible moment. We had fears that we would lose you, too.'

'I guessed that from the strain showing in my uncle's face.'

'You are on the mend, now, anyway. Don't try to talk too much. I will come and see you tomorrow.'

He left the room quite abruptly. After he had gone I lay thinking about one thing and another until, exhausted, I slept.

The following morning I felt much better. Tina greeted me cheerfully and with her assistance I washed and changed into a clean nightgown.

'What a time we've had in this house, Miss Marnie, with doctors coming and going all hours. Never mind, nobody minds at all as long as you are better . . . '

In spite of the general rejoicing, though, after the first feeling of euphoria, a black depression seemed to settle over me. I tried to conceal it as much as possible.

During the time that I had been critically ill I had dreamed of Carl von Oldenburg, and in my dream he had come to my bedside and held my hand. It was so vivid that I could scarcely believe that it had not been real. The memory of it left me with a sense of sadness; of emotional insecurity and something else which I could not put into words. I knew from what my uncle had said that Alistair had been very attentive when I was so ill. I felt a mixture of gratitude and compassion for him; I also had a feeling of friendship towards him, but beyond that I felt little.

In some strange way my sickness had made me realise that I could never marry Alistair. I had no doubt that he would make a very good husband for someone, but not for me. The more I pondered on this, the more certain I became that I should break off our engagement. That would not be pleasant, nor would it be easy.

Tina brought some letters up to my room, letters from friends and acquaintances who had heard of my illness. Among them was a letter from Isabel, written from Cromer.

'Dear Marnie,' it ran. 'As you can see, I am staying in Cromer with my Aunt Hester. Both Mama and Dr. Harlow have written to tell me of your illness. I hope you make a speedy recovery. I am sorry I have not seen you since the night of the ball, but I have been suffering with my nerves. Dr. Harlow thought that a change would be beneficial to me, so you see I am here on 'doctor's orders'. I understand that you called at the house shortly before you were ill, but I was lying in a darkened room with a headache. I was really prostrate. I have been very upset, too, to hear of Dr. Harlow's father's death. I am hoping to recover my health and spirits here, and I hope you soon recover yours, although, naturally, yours will take rather longer. I send you my best wishes. As ever, Isabel.'

What a peculiar letter, I thought, putting it away. It was so brief and non-committal — a sort of duty letter; well, more of a note, really. So she was in Cromer on doctor's orders, according to her. I thought her recent behaviour had been odd in the extreme. She had been a constant caller at our house ever since her parents had bought Hove House. Now she appeared to have changed towards me and the change had been sudden. Her brief letter did nothing to dispel my depression.

Alistair visited me daily, sometimes in the afternoon, sometimes in the evening. He would sit at the bedside, his hand clasped lightly over mine. There was no doubt that he was pleased by my progress, but somehow things were different between us. In my heart I knew that they had started to be different before I was ill. It was true that I'd had doubts about the wisdom of becoming engaged to him, right from the time he had first mentioned marriage. He, however, had appeared to have no such uncertainties; his very sureness that we were doing the right thing had made me stifle my own feelings of indecision. I sensed that he no longer felt the same confidence in our future together.

One evening I was out of bed and sitting in a chair when he came. Dr. Hargreaves and my uncle said that I could be allowed to do this for a short time every day. Alistair never stayed for more than a quarter of an hour at a time. As soon as he entered the room and greeted me I asked if it was going to be another brief visit. He looked startled.

'I didn't think you would want me to stay very long, Marnie.'

'No? You are regarding these visits as professional?' I hated the sharp edge to my voice, but I felt there were things he was not being open about.

'I don't believe in tiring patients.'

'Then you need not stay long. I am very sorry that you have had so much trouble lately. I know that I have added to it.'

'Your illness has been a great anxiety, naturally.' He sat down opposite me in front of the coal fire, as the nights were growing chilly now.

'Alistair,' I heard myself saying, 'would you like to be released from our engagement?'

'Released?' The blank look on his face was superseded almost immediately by a different expression altogether. One of relief — of hope. I took his ring off my finger. He watched me without speaking. I handed it back to him.

'It's best, I think,' I said. 'Best for both of us.'

He began to remonstrate. 'You are not yourself, dear. When you feel better you may think differently — ' he broke off. The lack of conviction in his voice must have been as obvious to him as it was to me.

'It is not necessary for you to say things like that,' I said quietly. 'For you to ask to be released from our engagement would not be the gentlemanly thing to do. I understand that. But do not pretend that you are sorry.'

For a moment he made no reply. He looked completely nonplussed. Then he spoke. 'In view of — well — everything, Marnie, I think that you are right. I'm very grateful that you have been so frank with me. Things have been very trying lately.'

I watched him slip the engagement ring into his pocket. The air seemed to be full of unspoken words. I wanted them to remain unspoken, too. I didn't want the whys and wherefores of our broken engagement to be dragged out and examined. It had ended quietly in a matter-of-fact way and, most curious of all, with seemingly no regrets on either side.

'You know, of course, Marnie, that I will always admire you and want to be friends.' He rose from the chair.

'Of course,' I echoed. 'And I'm very grateful for the way you have helped care for me during my illness.'

'I was only too pleased to do what I could. You know that.'

For a moment he stood hesitating, as if he wanted to say more. Instead, he dropped a swift kiss on my forehead and left the room, pausing at the door to give me a little wave.

I slipped off my *peignoir*, walked slowly over to the bed and climbed into it again. I lay back on the pillows. It was all over. Whatever the future had in store for me, it would not be shared with Alistair. I was not unaware of his good qualities. Indeed, I never had been. He was kind and conscientious, dedicated to his profession and good-looking, with pleasing manners, too. I knew that, if I had not returned his ring, he would have married me and gallantly made the best of things, even though his feelings towards me had changed. How strange it all was, though, that things could end like this so quickly. He had made one half-hearted protest and then accepted the situation.

About twenty minutes after Alistair had left me there was another tap at the door.

'Come in,' I called, and my uncle entered the room. As soon as I saw his face, concerned and tender, I knew that Alistair had taken it upon himself to tell my uncle the news.

'How are you, my dear?' He sat down.

'I'm feeling much stronger. I've been sitting up for quite a long time,' I said, making my voice cheerful. Uncle Peter reached out and patted my hand.

'Alistair has told me about the broken engagement, Marnie, so you don't need to worry on that score. He thought it was better coming from him, under the circumstances. It was no great surprise to me.'

'Oh!' I was taken aback. I had thought that it would be quite a blow to my uncle, particularly in view of the recent engagement ball.

'When people recover from a bad illness, they often see things very clearly. I have always thought Alistair a fine young man. He has many qualities to recommend him. But that does not mean that I would put pressure on you to marry him.'

At his kind and understanding words I began to weep, quietly and bitterly. But the tears were not because I was no longer engaged to marry Alistair. I was weeping for Carl von Oldenburg, my lost love. I was weeping because I still loved him, even though I knew that he had murdered his wife; murdered her with me in mind. I had tried to cut him out of my life and I had failed.

Strangely enough, my uncle did not stay in the room and comfort me. He crept out and left me to my sorrow. He must have sensed that it was the right thing to do. I wanted to be left alone.

13

It was autumn and the last of the summer visitors had left Southsands, which was preparing for its winter sleep. Fear of a diphtheria epidemic had sent a number of families home before the end of the season. Fortunately, their panic had been unfounded, although there were still a few cases in the neighbourhood.

The friendship between my uncle and Miss Hetherington had deepened, and, although I had not broached the subject to him, nor he to me, I felt that marriage must be in his mind. This was confirmed one breezy October day, when he told me that he had decided to retire.

'Well,' I said slowly, assimilating the news as I poured tea for us in the drawing room, 'it's about time. And what will become of the practice?'

'I shall sell it. There is a Dr. Clarke interested, someone Dr. Hargreaves knows well.'

'But what about Alistair?' I had seen little of him socially since I had broken off our engagement.

My uncle looked uncomfortable. 'He's leaving Southsands, Marnie. He's going into partnership with his brother in Edinburgh. There are other factors, too — but I expect you have heard about them.'

'Heard what? I haven't heard anything. Remember, Uncle, I've been convalescent for weeks, but staying in and resting.'

'Do you know that Isabel is back from Cromer?'

'As a matter of fact, no. Isabel behaved in rather a strange manner at the ball and refused to see me when I called at the house to see how she was. I had a brief note from her when she heard that I had diphtheria and that's all. I've been cut off from the outside world for weeks and quite a lot of people are afraid of infection long after the disease has gone.'

'Yes, that's true, Marnie, but who can blame them?'

'Nobody, I suppose. Not that I've minded. I haven't wanted any company except yours and Miss Hetherington's.'

This was quite true. Weakness and listlessness had followed in the wake of diphtheria. I had felt like staying at home and hiding away. I had been deserted by Isabel, and Alistair was no longer my fiancé. To kindly enquiries from other friends in Southsands I instructed Tina that I was still not well enough for visitors. I spent many hours sitting by the fire, wondering what I would do with my life, wondering, too, what was going on at Schloss Beissel.

Uncle Peter leaned forward, picked up the poker and prodded a piece of coal with elaborate care. 'I believe Isabel and Alistair have a mind to get married.'

I caught my breath momentarily and my uncle cast an anxious glance in my direction.

'It's alright,' I said, finding my composure again. 'I've an idea they realised they were in love before the ball. I think Isabel was attracted to Alistair right from the start. If she accompanied us anywhere she would joke about playing gooseberry, but I think I was doing that, perhaps before Alistair realised it. I don't mind. I suppose things got too much for Isabel at the engagement ball. I can see a lot of things now. When I called at Isabel's house and she wouldn't receive me, I happened to see Alistair drive there shortly afterwards. He didn't see me, but I sat in the park and timed his call. He had been there for an hour when I walked back home. He never mentioned how long he had stayed there, so I had certain suspicions before I was ill.'

'I see.' Uncle Peter rubbed his chin thoughtfully. 'It's best, anyway, that he should go back to Scotland. There is bound to be some gossip in Southsands. He can marry Isabel and take her up there to make a fresh start.'

'Yes. I'm sure they'll be happy,' I said.

'And there's another matter, Marnie.'

Uncle Peter cleared his throat and poked the fire again. He gave me a nervous glance.

'More tea?' I enquired, wondering what was coming next.

'Er, no — I mean, yes, please — '

I poured him out another cup. He stirred the sugar in carefully, then put it down without taking one sip. 'It's about Miss Hetherington. We've grown very fond of one another — very fond. I regard her highly, Marnie. The fact is — well — I'm considering asking her to marry me. Are you surprised?'

I smiled reassuringly, he looked so anxious. 'Not really.'

'And you don't mind? I've been rather concerned as to what you would think of the idea.'

'I think it's a splendid idea. If you marry Miss Hetherington, I'll be happy for you both. I shall have to make plans of my own then, I suppose.'

'But, my dear, you will make your home with us, naturally.'

'I don't know about that. I shall have to see.'

My uncle looked worried. 'Marnie, your happiness is of paramount importance to me . . . I would do anything to make you happy — anything — ' He looked so anxious that I felt very moved. 'I know you are not happy,' he added in a low voice.

'Don't worry about me so,' I said lightly. 'I'm thankful to be getting better. You can carry on with your plans and I shall think about my own plans for the future while I am still convalescent.'

That night I was a long time going to sleep. In a way it was a relief to hear my uncle intended to propose to Miss Hetherington. I had little doubt as to the outcome. I felt sure that they would be very happy together. My own future loomed ahead of me. In spite of Uncle Peter's kind words and, much as I liked Miss Hetherington, somehow I could not see myself living permanently with them. It would be my home, yes, but it seemed to me that the best thing for me to do under the circumstances was to take another position as a governess. Perhaps in England, perhaps on the Continent. Not in Germany, though. I would never go back there again.

That same week Alistair called in to see me one wet, blustery evening. After greeting me and enquiring after my health, he told me rather hesitantly that Isabel was back at home.

'I know. Uncle told me.'

'I think she would like to visit you, Marnie.' He looked both nervous and embarrassed.

'She is at liberty to do so.' I replied.

'Yes, but there are things to explain. It involves me as well as Isabel.'

'I think I know what you mean. I think you want to tell me that you and Isabel are in love. It's not really a surprise.'

'Oh.' There was relief on his handsome face. 'It was something which neither of us could help,' he went on. 'It was a dreadful position for Isabel to be in. She was afraid of hurting you; she was most unhappy. I had told her that I could not go back on my word to you and she understood. She had to hide her own true feelings and try to appear cheerful. It was a dreadful effort for her to attend our engagement ball. And she simply could not face you afterwards — '

'Well, she can face me now,' I said quietly. 'I hope you'll both be very happy. I hear you are going back to Edinburgh to live.'

'Yes. My brother and I will carry on the practice between us.'

'I expect that is the way your father would have wanted it.'

'Yes . . . and you, Marnie, have you made any plans for the future?'

I knew that he felt slightly guilty because I had released him from our engagement and because he had every hope of being happy with Isabel. He wanted to think that life was going to offer me something, too.

'Not yet,' I replied cheerfully. 'I'm quite sure that I shall find something to do, as soon as I am strong enough. And of course I shall be pleased to see Isabel.'

Alistair stood up. 'I must go now. You are very understanding, Marnie.' He bent and kissed me lightly on the forehead. I felt a strange pang when he did so. He had kissed me like that the day I had broken off our engagement; a brotherly salute, nothing more. I had given him up to my friend. It was true that I did not love him, but I envied him the prospect of his happiness with Isabel. I envied Isabel, too, for the same reason.

Later that week she called to see me. Dressed in a delightful grey outfit, she looked adorably pretty and radiantly happy. We embraced each other; a very quick embrace, but it assured us that all was well again. She sat down and wiped her eyes with a lace-edged handkerchief. We were both a bit emotional.

'It's been an impossible situation, Marnie,' she said, twisting her handkerchief nervously. 'I couldn't see any way out. I was acting a lie. And then I found out that Alistair had fallen in love with me. I knew that he still intended to marry you, though — '

'It's all worked out for the best,' I said calmly. 'I expect there will be a bit of gossip about it in Southsands, but that doesn't matter.'

'But you're sure everything is well with you, Marnie? You must have had a terrible time, being so ill with diphtheria.'

'It was most unpleasant.'

'You've lost your colour and you've gone so thin . . . but I mean, are things alright, apart from still not being fully recovered?'

I smiled. 'Don't feel so guilty,' I said lightly.

'I didn't know that one could fall in love with — well, someone who belonged to someone else,' she continued. 'I couldn't believe it — and when

343

at last I told Mama, she was horrified. She said it was dreadful, feeling like that about my best friend's fiancé. Then, when she saw how desperately unhappy I was, she realised it wasn't just a passing attraction. I blurted out the truth to her at your engagement ball — you can't imagine how awful everything was that evening. I had to go home, I simply had to . . . '

'There's no need for these explanations, Isabel. People do fall in love unexpectedly; love can't be commanded.'

She looked relieved. 'I was afraid you would hate me.'

'Hate you? Of course not.'

'When I was at Cromer I heard that you were very ill. I should have written you a longer letter, but I couldn't bring myself to. I thought of Alistair, sitting beside your bed — caring for you . . . ' she broke off, her dark eyes begging me to understand, and, because of my own bitter emotional experiences, I did understand. I could gauge the intensity of her feelings, her longings, her jealousy, everything. Although we were the same age, I suddenly felt immeasurably older.

'Mama is very fond of Alistair — she has always liked him. But she is afraid that people will gossip unkindly about me and say that I took him from you.'

'I'll stop the gossips,' I assured her. 'I'll dance at your wedding, Isabel.'

'Oh, Marnie, you are wonderful — ' she broke off and wiped her eyes again. I rang the bell for Tina to bring tea in.

When Isabel left the house some time later she seemed to radiate happiness. I reflected that it must be a tremendous relief to her that our friendship had survived. It was true that I did not blame her for what had happened; she had not set out to steal Alistair's love. There was no doubt that she adored him. Perhaps he had suspected that my feelings were not as intense as they should have been. He had been right about that, anyway. After Isabel had gone I sat down at the piano and let my hands stray idly across the keys. As I did so the door opened and my uncle appeared.

'My dear! How long have you been sitting alone?'

'Not long. I've had Isabel here visiting me.'

My uncle looked extremely nervous. He gave a short cough. 'There are one or two matters I would like to discuss with you, Marnie,' he said.

I rose from the piano and sat down by the fire with my uncle opposite me. 'Yes?' I said.

He warmed his hands in front of the blaze. 'Well, Miss Hetherington and I have reached an understanding. We hope to marry in the spring.'

'Congratulations, Uncle. I'm so happy for you.' I leaned forward and gave him a swift kiss.

'There is another matter, though — ' he broke off.

'Yes? Go on,' I said encouragingly.

'When you were ill, my dear, you were delirious. You weren't aware of it, of course. I heard certain things . . . ' he paused.

I could feel my heart beginning to thump painfully. 'Go on,' I said.

'You talked quite a lot of Germany and that schloss. And quite a lot of . . . ' he paused again. I could feel the blood rising to my face.

'You talked of Count von Oldenburg. You asked for him — '

'Why are you telling me this?' I interrupted, trembling with mortification. To have heard me say these things was bad enough, but to tell me about it was even worse. It was so unlike my uncle, too.

'Because, Marnie, I understood so many things then. There was such a lot that I suspected when you returned home, but your poor aunt was ill and you did not talk about your life at the schloss. When you became engaged to Alistair I thought that, whatever it was, you had got over it. When you had diphtheria, I knew differently. And I'm afraid Alistair heard you calling for

347

another man, too.'

'Oh,' I exclaimed, acutely embarrassed. It could not have been very pleasant for him; after all, he had been engaged to marry me at the time, even though his heart had been with Isabel. Whatever Alistair suspected, though, he would forever keep silent.

'When you were recovering and had broken off your engagement, I wrote to von Oldenburg.'

'Uncle!' I cried, confounded. 'You didn't!'

'I did, I'm afraid.'

'You had no right to, then! You had no right to interfere with my affairs like that!' I was trembling with anger and shame. 'You have always said how wrong it is to interfere,' I continued bitterly. 'How could you?'

'Because I wanted you to have a chance of happiness! There are times when one simply can't stand to one side. My dear child, I find the idea of your unhappiness quite unbearable! Yes, I have corresponded with this Count

— in a mixture of German and English. Marnie — ' he reached out and clasped my hand. 'He loves you! He is coming to see you — '

I sprang up, wrenching my hand away, oblivious of the hurt look in his eyes. 'I will not receive him! There are reasons — things which you do not understand. There are other things besides love in the world, things like honour and — and decent behaviour. You do not know the facts.'

'Are you sure that you know them?' he asked quietly.

'They are — the circumstances are too difficult to discuss,' I replied after a slight hesitation. 'It is connected with the death of the Countess . . . ' I broke off, remembering that night of horror, remembering the taut whiteness of the Count's face as he bent over the dead body of his wife. 'I can't talk about it.'

'He is coming to see you, Marnie, anyway. He will be arriving in England some time next week. I am sorry if I have done the wrong thing, but promise me that you will at least receive him.'

'Very well,' I said. 'But that is all I can promise.' I felt a raging inward anger, not just with my uncle, but with myself for talking about the Count in my delirium.

'I do understand that he was a married man up to the time of that tragic shooting,' said my uncle gently. 'Believe me, I would not judge you harshly for falling in love with a man who was already tied to another. His wife's death was an unexpected event, a terrible shock, and immediately afterwards you were called back to England because of your aunt's health. But all that is in the past, dear. It was twelve months ago; you could renew your acquaintanceship without undue comment.'

'It's not a simple thing like that. It's extremely complicated . . . ' Even as I spoke, the longing for Carl von Oldenburg rose up in me with a fierce urgency. I had tried — how I had tried — to crush it, but to no avail. If only he had denied shooting his wife . . . I sat down again because my legs were weak and trembling. How would I face the Count now? What had my uncle told him? I tried to compose myself.

'Asking the Count to come here could be very painful and embarrassing for me,' I said. 'Didn't you think of that?'

'You must know I would think of everything. But from the letters which I have received from him, I do not think that he would cause you pain if he could possibly help it. I am the one who invited him here, so you are at liberty to be angry with me, I suppose.'

'It's too late now, if he is already on his way.'

'I'm sorry. I can see now what a shock it's been to you.' My uncle looked crestfallen. 'Well, I wanted to do *something*. I've never interfered like this in my life.'

A suspicion crossed my mind. 'Does Miss Hetherington know about this?' I asked.

He looked guilty. 'Well, as a matter of fact, she does. She's very fond of you, Marnie, and she thought it was the right thing to do, too.'

'How strange,' I said. 'Both you and Miss Hetherington are all for not interfering with other people's lives, but where my life is concerned it seems to be different.'

Uncle Peter looked so hurt that I softened towards him. 'I'm sorry, Uncle,' I said, 'I know that you and Miss Hetherington mean well. I just wish that you had not done this.'

'It was a step in the dark, I admit. But I'll reserve my judgement until later.'

We played a game of bezique, but I was too upset and excited to concentrate. I went to bed with my head in a whirl. He was coming to see me; he was coming to England, to Southsands! Emotions were boiling up inside me; love for him and fear and hatred, too. Fear of my own feelings and of the unknown quality within him which had made him shoot Maria. Hatred of his ideas; his fanatical pride in the family name; his acceptance of Georg as Charlotte's future husband. Despite all this, though, I had cried out for him in my delirium . . .

A few days later a letter came addressed to me, postmarked London. I had seen the Count's pointed, Gothic handwriting before, during the time I had been at the schloss. Now once again I found myself gazing at it. It was just a short note, written in English.

'My Dearest Love, — ' it began. The painful tears pricked my eyes. 'I have taken the liberty to accept your uncle's invitation to call at your house. I am greatly sorry to hear of your illness. I will travel to Southsands in two days. My greets to you and to your good uncle. Carl von Oldenburg.'

Why hadn't he written a longer letter in German? But no, it was better as it was. We were at the breakfast table and I told my uncle that the Count would be at Southsands in a couple of days.

'Well, upon my soul! He certainly

hasn't wasted any time.'

I pushed my plate away. The idea of eating was nauseating. So many repressed emotions seemed to have been released in me by the sight of that handwriting. He was coming — he was coming! I felt hot and shivery at the same time.

Uncle Peter patted my hand. 'I want to meet him very much,' he said quietly.

When he had gone out on his morning rounds I went up to my room and sat and looked at myself in the dressing-table mirror. I looked paler and thinner than when I had been Charlotte's governess at the schloss. I remembered how I had tried to change things in the schoolroom; how I had defied the Countess and sought to give Charlotte the education which progressive middle-class parents were giving their daughters in England. How young I had been; an age of experience seemed to lie between that rather arrogant self-willed girl and the person I now was. And yet, I was not so much older. Perhaps, though, I was wiser.

Whatever he says, I shall send him away, I thought. Yet, even though I was angry with myself for doing it, I scrutinised my wardrobe and decided which dress I would wear when he called. Would he dine with us? That would depend on me entirely. I knew that Uncle Peter would respect my feelings on these matters.

The next two days passed. I remained outwardly calm, but inwardly in a turmoil. I found myself doing endless, small, unnecessary tasks; doing anything and everything to keep myself occupied. Again and again I took out that short letter and read it, although I knew the few words off by heart. The following morning, just after my uncle had gone out on his rounds, Tina walked into the breakfast room and announced that there was a gentleman to see me.

'A *foreign* gentleman, Miss Marnie.' Her eyes were wide with amazement and curiosity. She handed me his card.

Yes, it was the Count!

'He's in the drawing room'

'Very well, Tina. I shall join him there.'

She left the room and I took a deep breath while my heart beat frantically. I felt suffocated. Remembering the ways of the schloss, I had thought that things would have been more formal; that Heinrich would have called with the Count's visiting card in the first instance. Because he must have Heinrich with him.

I glanced down at my plain grey morning gown and gave my hair a quick pat. Then I went to the drawing room where the door had been left slightly open. I had thought over and over again the way I would greet him when he came; kindly, perhaps, but coolly, distantly. I would make him realise that he was not there at my invitation. I had not reckoned with the effect his presence would have on me. I closed the door quietly behind me and we were alone.

'Marnie!' He was by my side in a

couple of strides, holding out both hands. I had a swift impression of his blue eyes and the suffering in them and the leanness of his face. He was dressed in mourning. His hands clasped mine.

'Good day, I — I hope I see you well, Your Excellency,' I stammered, trying to make his visit as formal as possible.

'It is you who have been ill,' he replied, fumbling for the words in English in the old, enchanting way. It moved me unbearably.

'Please be seated.' I indicated a chair. 'I trust you had a good journey.'

'It was a good journey because I was coming to see you,' he replied simply, in German now. We sat down on opposite sides of the coal fire. How strange it was to see him at our fireside instead of in front of a great fireplace with burning pine longs sending forth their fragrance. How small and insignificant our house must seem to him. He was eyeing me keenly. I gripped the arms of the chair to try and stop my hands from trembling.

'You are paler than I remember,' he said quietly. 'And frailer, too. Your uncle wrote that you had been very ill indeed.'

'I am better now. How is Charlotte?'

'She is not at the schloss. She is a pupil at the school which you used to attend, and which you recommended for her.'

'Oh!' I exclaimed, surprised, but pleased, too.

'She is much happier there. And Gertrud has retired and lives in Goppertal.'

For a while he did most of the talking, telling me how well Charlotte was doing at school and how work had continued in the garden which had been neglected for so many years. I asked him where Heinrich was and he replied that he was waiting outside in the hired carriage.

I rang the bell for Tina and asked her to bring coffee. I also suggested that Heinrich should be taken into the kitchen for a hot drink.

'I doubt if our coffee will be much to your taste,' I told the Count.

'It will be to my taste if you hand it to me,' he replied gallantly.

There was a silence between us and I was thankful when Tina arrived with the coffee.

'I hope you do not think it is too bad,' I said, pouring the Count a cup and handing it to him.

'I find it excellent.' He set his cup down on the little table and adopted a more purposeful air. 'You have had a sad time since you returned to England. Your aunt died, and I am very sorry. Your uncle told me in a letter.'

'Yes,' I said. 'And you have lost your mother,'

'So you know? How do you know that?'

'By accident, really. I have been teaching German at my old school in Southsands, filling in a temporary vacancy caused by the teacher having to go back to Germany for a while because of her father's illness. She returned, bringing some newspapers, one of which has an account of your mother's death. I was very sorry to read it.'

'She is not suffering now,' he said quietly. 'And the past dies with her. Marnie, *liebling*, there are things which I must tell you. I know that you had to leave the schloss in a hurry, but you left with a cloud hanging over everything.'

'I would have left in any case, even if I had not received that telegram,' I said in a low voice.

'Please, let me speak. There were things which I could not tell you at the time; dark secrets which I could share with no one.' His unwavering gaze was upon me. I did not speak, remembering that painful scene between us when I had asked him to deny murdering his wife and he had not done so.

'Now I can share these things with you,' he went on. 'A few days after the shooting my mother confessed to me that she had done it. At first I thought that her mind was going; that her illness had affected her. Then she opened a secret panel in her room and showed me the pistol which she had concealed there ... ' he broke off, unable to continue.

There was no sound in the room except for the ticking of the ormolu clock on the mantle-shelf. The Count composed himself and began to speak again.

'She explained that, as she knew that she was going to die she decided to get rid of her daughter-in-law first. It was as big as the shock of Maria's death — my own mother — a murderess!'

I had been trembling ever since I had set eyes on him; now I began to feel faint as well.

'Your mother ... the Countess Adelaide!' I gasped.

'Yes. She had never liked Maria. There were many reasons for that, but I won't go into them now. What really drove her to murder was finding out about Maria and von Schilsky. My mother hated loose morals and Maria's behaviour outraged her. I could not believe it at first when my mother told me what she knew. I trusted Maria implicitly. It is natural for a man to do so; she was my own wife; she was Countess Maria von Oldenburg.'

Even now I caught the echo of wounded pride in his voice.

'That Maria could have a lover under the very roof of the schloss was more than my mother could stand. Apparently she had known of their affair for some time and kept silent. Can you understand the predicament I was in when she confessed to me?'

'Yes,' I said. 'I understand.' My voice sounded hoarse and strange.

'Difficult as it was to believe at first, I finally realised that she was telling the truth. She was responsible for Maria's death. It was like living through a nightmare. My first thought was to get that pistol out of the schloss and as far away as possible. I crept out early in the morning and put it in the hollow tree for the time being. Later that day I removed it and made sure it was disposed of for ever. I told my mother that she must keep silent about it, if not for her own sake, for the sake of Charlotte and myself. She was in a terrible state; it was as if she had only just realised what she had done. The pistol had been given to her by my father for her protection many years before. I never knew she had it. I tried to calm her, but it was very difficult. As for my own feelings — the shock of knowing that my own mother had been capable of committing murder! That she had killed my own wife!'

He broke off again, unable to continue for a few minutes.

'My mother had been brought up as a devout Catholic, but the von Olden-burgs were staunch Protestants. She was determined to marry my father, so she lapsed from the faith of Rome, but shortly before she died she told me that she wanted to be reconciled with the Church. I respected her wishes and a priest was brought to the house. She confessed to him and I asked him to stay with her, as she was so ill. The following day he administered the Last Rites and she died about two hours afterwards. Charlotte was at the *Damenstift*, so she had to be brought home for the funeral.'

Something in the quiet, simple way he was telling me all this moved me unbearably. I could feel the tears running down my cheeks. How dreadfully he had suffered.

'It would have been more bearable if you had not accused me of shooting Maria. If you had trusted me more; had not tried to compel me to confess or deny it. It was a great shock to me that you had found the pistol; that you had witnessed me putting it in the hollow tree. I was in a difficult situation. If only you had trusted me, Marnie. But looking back, I asked a great deal from you.'

I was unable to speak. I knew that he was telling me the truth about Maria's death. All he asked of me was that I should trust him, and I had not done so.

'I am asking you now to believe what I have just told you. Nothing else; only that.'

'I believe you,' I said at last, in a low voice. 'I am sorry that I did not trust you at the time. Perhaps you will forgive me.'

'Forgive you! I must surely ask you to forgive me for all the sadness I brought into your life. It was a great grief to me that you could not find it in your heart to trust me; to know that I was incapable of committing a crime like that. Yet, in a way, I could not blame you.'

How could I ever have suspected him of such a crime? It was hard to imagine that his mother could have taken a human life, even though she had disliked her daughter-in-law intensely. Although Carl von Oldenburg had saved Maria from disgrace by marrying her, still she had taken a lover while pleading ill-health to her husband. Any mother would have been outraged by such behaviour, and if she was a woman who knew her own life was drawing to a close, she could well have been moved to the ultimate crime.

'My mother was very fond of you,' went on the Count. 'She was sad when I told her you had gone away. She said the schloss was a better place when you were there.'

He suddenly knelt down on the hearthrug and clasped my hands in his. 'It is true, Marnie. I know that you were engaged to marry another man, because your uncle told me so in a letter, but he said that you had broken it off. That was when he first wrote to me. I thank God that I am not too late. A day has not passed since you left the schloss when I have not longed for you and grieved for you; but I dare not write. And Charlotte — poor child — '

'I know,' I said, finding my voice at last. 'Do you think I haven't grieved and worried about Charlotte? It has been terrible.'

Then I felt his arms around me, his lips pressed to mine. The emotion of that moment was indescribable; the warmth, the closeness, the ecstasy. It was like jumping off a high mountain and finding myself able to fly. It was like being a Rain Bird, and I told him so as soon as he released me from that first embrace.

'Ah, yes,' he said smiling. 'I remember being madly jealous that night when you were chosen to be the Rain Bird. I came hurrying after you and Georg.'

'It was lucky for me that you did,' I said. 'What has happened to him, by the way?'

'Nothing, really. He is as ever. But as for Charlotte marrying him — well, that is up to you, *liebling*.'

He helped me out of my chair and we sat together on the sofa, holding each other in a close embrace.

'How is it up to me?' I asked.

He bent and kissed me, very slowly. 'You must know that, Marnie.'

Yes, I knew it. I knew that he wanted me to marry him, become his Countess and live in Schloss Beissel with him. And he hoped, too, for children of his own; for at least one son to carry on his name. He did not say all this, but I knew it. And I knew that I wanted it, too.

'Tell me that you care,' he whispered. 'That you truly love me, in spite of all that we have been through; in spite of the fact that you became engaged to another man. I love you so much. Please marry me, Marnie.'

The love in his eyes and the sadness in his voice seemed to pluck at my very heart strings.

'I love you with all my heart.' At last I said the words which I had never thought I would say to him. As I spoke a sudden panic rose in me. I loved him, but the strangeness, the foreignness of life at the schloss! The things which I neither liked nor understood . . .

'But you wouldn't want anything changing,' I said. 'And there are things which I would want changing. I can't help my nature — '

'When we are married we will solve these problems together. We will have things more like your English ways — ' he broke off and thought for a moment. 'We will change the plumbing,' he said solemnly. 'I will have running water laid on in the schloss and — er — other things done for you. And Charlotte will be a comfort to you. And even if we do not have a son of our own, she will not be compelled to marry Georg.'

'Oh!' I exclaimed, astonished. 'But what of the family name? What of the honour of the von Oldenburgs?'

'Perhaps in the past we have thought too much of honour and too little of happiness,' he said. 'All I want now is happiness, Marnie. I know that my relations will think it strange indeed that I should marry an English governess when I could choose a wife from an aristocratic German family. But I do not care for their opinion. We love each other and I want what I have never had, the chance to live happily with the wife of my choice; one who loves me and whom I truly love. I did my best to be a good husband to Maria,

369

but it was a marriage of convenience. Some day I will tell you about it, but not now. All that matters now is our love for each other.'

I could feel myself trembling in his arms. I knew that nothing would ever part us again; we belonged to each other, in spite of our different backgrounds. Love mocked at such things.

'I'll take you out on the mountainside,' he whispered. 'We can listen to the bells together.'

As he spoke I could see Schloss Beissel in my mind's eye. A fairy-tale castle set on towering heights, guarding the little town of Goppertal far below. I could hear the bells echoing; could remember vividly the exhilarating clearness of the air. I suddenly longed to breathe it again; I yearned for the smell of pine forests, for the sight of a wood cutter; for the sound of German *Lieder* played on an old fiddle in a hunting lodge.

'We'll get married as soon as possible,' I said softly. 'I've been away a long time. I want to go home now, Carl.'

A FRAGILE SANCTUARY

Roberta Grieve

When Jess Fenton refuses to have her disabled sister locked away, her employer turns them out of their cottage. Wandering the country lanes in search of work, they find unlikely sanctuary at a privately run home for the mentally ill — the very place that Jess had vowed her sister would never enter. As she settles into her new job, Jess finds herself falling in love with the owner of Chalfont Hall, even as she questions his motivation in running such a place.

SHIFTING SANDS

Shelagh Fenton

Ruth's father tells her that he has taken on Paul as a business partner, and whilst being obliged to co-operate with him, Ruth's reaction is to feel a deep distrust for a man she hardly knows. However, she comes to trust him and love him as they work together to track down her cousin Melanie, who has disappeared. Then Paul saves Ruth's life at serious cost to himself . . . just as they finally locate Melanie who is in great danger . . .

ONCE UPON A TIME

Zelma Falkiner

City girl Meredith plans to write a novel in the peace and quiet of the country, but finds her chosen retreat is over-run by a film production company. Despite her best intentions, she is soon lured from her story-telling into a make-believe world of early Australia, with handsome, bearded bush-rangers on horseback, and women in long skirts, boots and gingham bonnets. But in the real world, a little girl is in danger . . .

A TOUCH OF MAGIC

June Gadsby

Lorna is trying to rebuild her life after the war that robbed her of her husband and her son of a father he never knew. However, eleven-year-old Simon refuses to accept that Max is dead. Lorna does not believe in miracles, but it is Christmas and all Simon asks is the chance to see the place where his father's plane crashed. In the dense Basque forest, a man called Olentzero brings a touch of magic back into their lives . . .